LOOKING-GLASS JUSTICE

Recent Titles by Jeffrey Ashford from Severn House

THE COST OF INNOCENCE
AN HONEST BETRAYAL
MURDER WILL OUT
A WEB OF CIRCUMSTANCES

Writing as Roderic Jeffries

DEFINITELY DECEASED

LOOKING-GLASS JUSTICE

Jeffrey Ashford

This first world edition published in Great Britain 2001 by
SEVERN HOUSE PUBLISHERS LTD of
9–15 High Street, Sutton, Surrey SM1 1DF.
This first world edition published in the USA 2001 by
SEVERN HOUSE PUBLISHERS INC of
595 Madison Avenue, New York, N.Y. 10022.

British Library Cataloguing in Publication Data

Ashford, Jeffrey, 1926–
  Looking-glass justice
  1. Detective and mystery stories
  I. Title
  823.9'14 [F]

ISBN 0-7278-5613-8

Typeset by Palimpsest Book Production Ltd.,
Polmont, Stirlingshire, Scotland.
Printed and bound in Great Britain by
MPG Books Ltd., Bodmin, Cornwall.

One

The roof, even more dilapidated than the rest of the hut, had been inadequately repaired with palm fronds where the corrugated iron had rusted away, and a sudden stream of water splashed down within inches of Lynch's right knee. He hastily stood and moved the rickety chair to what, he optimistically hoped, would prove a drier area. He stared through the doorway at the sodden land that stretched down to the mangrove swamp, which tainted the air with the scent of decay. Beyond the mangroves was the sullen, mud-coloured river. Sailing up in the long, narrow boat, Togba had casually said in his fractured English that there were many, many snakes in the river. He could have had no idea of the fear his words would provoke. Lynch had an uncontrollable fear of snakes and from that moment his mind had been plagued by the vision of triangular, flattened heads with flickering, forked tongues and poisoned fangs reaching out of the water.

The rain stopped as abruptly as it had started. The ground steamed and the smell of decay increased although there was no appreciable breeze towards the hut. Unpleasant smells made him feel sick and he thought with increasing nostalgia of his spotlessly clean home, furnished with great taste.

There was a sudden outburst of ugly, chattering sound, similar to that which he'd heard earlier as Togba had steered up to the flimsy landing stage. Togba had said it was caused by a troop of monkeys. He hated monkeys.

1

They were said to have brought HIV into the world of humans.

Togba stepped into the doorway. 'They come.'

'How many of them are there?'

'Many, many.'

Perhaps he could not count beyond five. 'Bring the Dutchman here, but keep the rest outside.'

Togba disappeared. The minutes passed and then a tall, thin man, his gaunt face making him look older than he was, the straggly imperial beard doing nothing for his appearance, entered. 'Hullo, there. Great to see you.' Dijkstal's English was so idiomatic that it was sometimes difficult to remember he was a Dutchman.

Lynch came to his feet and Dijkstal shook his hand with continental enthusiasm. As soon as he could, he surreptitiously wiped his palm on the side of his trouser leg because the other's hand had been wet and this might have been from sweat rather than from rain.

'My name is Jan and yours is . . . ? Christian names make for friendship, don't you think?'

'Indeed,' agreed Lynch. Never lose a chance to promote a suggestion of trust since there was no better camouflage for distrust. 'Mine is Esme.'

'I don't think I have heard that before.'

'Probably not.'

'I like it.'

Lynch had hated it when his fellow schoolboys had jeered at him for having a name that was also a girl's.

'Shall I sit here?' Dijkstal settled on the only other chair, even more rickety and less comfortable than the one on which Lynch sat. 'Tell me, Esme, did the happy thought occur to you to bring a bottle, or perhaps two, of whisky from Freetown to cement our friendship?'

'I'm afraid it didn't.'

'A great pity. But perhaps by way of consolation, you can offer me a proper cigarette?'

'I don't smoke.'

'One man's virtue is another man's suffering . . . I will have to be content with what I have, always a difficult thing to do.' He brought a pack from his pocket, tapped out a cigarette.

'I can't stand smoke.'

'Then I will endeavour to send it all away from you. Rumour has it that these are made from dried camel shit imported from Saudi Arabia. I usually scorn rumours, but this one I am prepared to accept.'

'I'll remember to have a couple of bottles of Haig and a carton of cigarettes ready for when we meet again.'

'How very kind. And if the cigarettes could possibly be Chesterfield . . . However, we may first be presented with a problem.'

'How's that?'

'There has, does there not, Esme, have to be total frankness between us?'

'What else?' Almost anything. Total frankness was a passport to disaster.

'Then you will permit me to say this. However friendly we may find ourselves – perhaps I should say, already are – we have only just met. And because circumstances are what they are, I like to be certain about someone with whom I am about to do business before I do that business.'

'I might say the same.'

'Naturally. We are both sensible men. So let us find out how quickly our knowledge can wave aside all problems. Do you have generous financial backing?'

'Do you have the diamonds?'

'Of course.'

'Then I have the backing.'

'But is it heavy enough?'

'Are your diamonds good enough to warrant the backing I have?'

Dijkstal smiled; unfortunately, the shape of his lips made

a grimace of his smile. 'We circle each other like partners on the dance floor who do not move closer for fear the other suffers from BO.'

It was years since Lynch had heard anyone use that expression. It disgusted him.

'Let me be the first to get closer because I have no such fear. My interest lies in diamonds which are so free of faults that most can truly be called perfect.'

'I have enough weight to buy as many as you have to sell – provided the price is right.'

'Cash. US dollars.'

'Not cash. The sum we will agree will be deposited in a bank which does not concern itself with where the money comes from or goes to. I will call the bank on satellite telephone and authorize them to make an immediate electronic transfer to whatever bank, in whatever country, you name. We will wait a short while and then you can use my phone to call your bank and make certain the transfer is complete. Since I cannot know what bank you'll choose, there can be no deception on my part.'

'As if I could think such a thing! Nevertheless, you are right, it is better to enjoy certainty even when there is complete trust.' Dijkstal dropped the cigarette stub on to the dirt floor, ground it out with the heel of his boot. 'What do you know about diamonds, Esme?'

'Nothing.'

'Then you will trust my judgement?'

'I would, naturally, but there are others who are small-minded and would suspect an archangel of lying.'

'There are always such people . . . How will you ensure that the diamonds are what I say they are?'

'I have someone back in Freetown who knows all there is to know about them.'

'No man can do that.'

'Then I will just say he can value one to the last dollar.'

'But does he understand his values?'

'How d'you mean?'

'A diamond is so much more than that which someone will pay to hang around a woman's neck. It is filled with mystery. It comes from deep within the earth – why? It is born of unimaginable pressures – how? Why does common carbon take ordinary light and turn this into dazzling beauty? How can it possess so much beauty when it is ice cold?'

Lynch wondered if the life Dijkstal led had begun to disturb his mind.

'You seem untroubled by the mysteries. Perhaps I will open your eyes a little.' He lit another cigarette, inhaled, coughed, hawked and spat on to the floor to Lynch's disgust. 'A year and a half ago, a worker in the B.S. brought—'

'B.S.?'

'The Bafi-Sewa drainage system which is where the diamondiferous gravel lies . . . He brought me a large rough diamond. For you, Esme, I am sure this would have appeared to be no more than a dull, greasy stone, but as I held it in the palm of my hand, I could glimpse the perfection that was waiting to be released. I must have shown my excitement, much as I tried to hide it, because this man demanded far more than I was prepared to pay. In the end, however, it became mine.'

Had the bargaining been long and fierce, or had a shot in the back of the head brought it to a quick close?

'Knowing nothing about diamonds, you cannot appreciate the anxieties and doubts that a man suffers, the decisions made and unmade, before he begins work. Are there flaws, to saw or to cleave, what cut – brilliant, rose, or some other? Using all the skills my years in Amsterdam have given me, I finally reached a decision. And weeks later, or was it months, I was looking at a brilliant cut fancy diamond that even if worn by the grandest noble lady would outshine her.'

'What's so fancy about it?'

Dijkstal smiled again. 'Fancy in this context means tinged with colour. This diamond is blood-red, the rarest of all colours, and is perhaps as large as any recorded. It is a shade under ten carats.'

'How big does that make it in actual size?'

'Compare it to a very small peach pit.'

'A what?'

'The space a very small peach stone occupies.'

English as taught by a bloody Dutchman! 'So what's it worth?'

'Red diamonds are often described as being virtually priceless.'

'An empty description. Everything has a price.'

'Real beauty does not suffer that disadvantage.'

'Until we have one, we can't talk.'

'It is not for sale.'

'If you think . . .'

'I think it is not for sale.'

After a brief pause, Lynch said: 'But what if it were?'

'Then one might talk about three million dollars.'

'You are obviously an optimist!'

'A realist. And perhaps I shall prove that to you. I will show you this matchless beauty when we meet here again in one week's time and arrange our business.'

When dealing with someone for whom suspicion was necessarily second nature, it was often wise to suggest the opposite to what was wanted. 'That would be interesting. But I suggest my hotel so that whisky and Chesterfields are to hand.'

'No.'

'But . . .'

'Here or nowhere.'

'You're condemning me to that bloody awful journey on the river again?'

'It is a picnic to the one I have to undertake.'

'Have it your way, then. But I hope to God I manage to survive getting here and back a second time.'

'The RFU have not recently been reported in the area.'

'But what about a week's time?'

'One cannot escape the future. You stand here and the future proves you should have stood there; you stand there and learn you should have stood here.' The cigarette had gone out when half smoked. Dijkstal threw it down on to the dirt, stood. 'I must leave if I am to be somewhere reasonably safe by dark. Night is the second most dangerous enemy . . . Goodbye, Esme, and I look forward very much to our next meeting here in a week's time. And should you remember to bring along a bottle or two of Scotch – please not the local brew, which may be compared to slurry – and some genuine cigarettes, it will be an even greater pleasure to greet you.'

Lynch followed Dijkstal out of the building. In the clearing, slumped on the sodden ground in two groups, were six men, dressed in jungle fatigues, each armed with an automatic rifle. Dijkstal gave a sharp order in Mende and reluctantly they came to their feet.

'You don't travel alone!' Lynch said.

'I have a dream which I intend to turn into reality.'

'A dream about what?'

'Leaving this hell-hole of a country and living somewhere where it's never stifling hot and humid, the food's edible, toes don't grow fungus between them, clothes don't go mouldy, and an unusual sound outside is the wind not the RFU looking for more hands and feet to slice off . . . Goodbye, Esme. I am happy that our friendship will prosper.' He shook hands with the same enthusiasm as before.

Lynch watched Dijkstal, followed by his armed guards, walk to the narrow path which led through the mangroves to the landing stage, which was in need of repair. He

7

remembered the snakes in the river and shivered, even as sweat further stained his shirt.

On Friday, Lynch returned to the Hôtel Splendide – had any name ever been more inappropriate? – after watching an old film in a cinema which had smelled of humans and the seeds many were forever chewing.

The reception clerk greeted him with a smile. 'Sir, he is here.'

'Who is?'

'He is, sir. Over here.' The clerk pointed across the foyer.

On the far side, seated on a settee whose cover was faded and worn, sat a woman overcome by boredom. Lynch remembered that the clerk's English invariably mistook both gender and direction.

He crossed to the settee. 'Carol?'

'I've been waiting here for hours,' she said petulantly. 'And this sofa's made of iron . . . The nasty little man behind the counter wouldn't let me into your room.'

Leaving her to carry her suitcase, which was obviously heavy, he led the way across to the lift. It wasn't working. He began to climb the stairs that curved around the lift shaft. By the first floor, he was short of breath, by the second, puffing, by the third, worrying about a heart attack. Recently, a specialist had advised him that his heart was still sound, but could hardly be expected to stay so unless he lost a great deal of weight. Had he not enjoyed good food to the extent he did, he might have been better able to insure his future.

He unlocked the door of his room and went in, knowing fresh irritation at the back of his right knee; because he carried too much flesh, he sweated heavily and various nooks of his body suffered a painful rash, no matter how often he showered. A local chemist had sold him at great expense some ointment that had proved totally useless.

She crossed to the settee, dropped the suitcase, sat. 'It was a bloody awful flight. Bumpy and kids were screaming all the way.'

'Children never do anything else.'

'The food was ghastly.'

'It usually is . . . I'm going to have a shower.'

'And you don't want me to soap you, right?'

'Why d'you say that?' he asked sharply.

She shrugged her shoulders – did he think anyone was going to mistake him for a Don Juan? 'Why have you got me out to this dump?'

'You'll be told.'

'Why can't you say now?'

'I'll tell you what you're not here for and that's to ask questions,' he said sharply. He crossed to the chest of drawers that was against the wall on the far side of the second bed. She aroused his sharp dislike. Early thirties trying to look in her twenties; blonde hair inexpertly dyed and badly styled; too much make-up; unsuitable costume jewellery; clothes that lacked all taste. A tart. But because most modern styles made women look like tarts, she should not draw attention to herself when she returned to England . . . He brought silk shirt and pants out of the second drawer. Silk was probably not the best material to wear in such a climate, but his skin demanded the luxury of its texture. He went through to the bathroom.

In the sitting room, Carol turned her head to look through the single, large window; the view was as depressing as that seen from her flat at home, yet in her naivety, she had thought to find in an exotic Freetown a temporary release from life . . .

She had more than enough experience to have already judged that behind Lynch's chosen appearance there lurked a mean and vicious character. It came home to her that she'd been a fool to agree to make the trip. But in truth she'd hardly been in a position to refuse. She'd been ill

9

for several weeks and trade had suffered, Norma was about to go to a new school so needed the uniform and all the expensive consumer accessories that would allow her to hold her head high, the landlady was demanding an increase in rent, and Maisie wanted more money to continue to act as her "housekeeper" . . .

Two

Frayne put the three sheets of paper, clipped together, in the folder. Tomorrow, he'd present to the other directors at their weekly get-together his pilot for an advertising campaign to boost the products of a locally based company. His ideas could be turned down, however good. Even the slightest hint of sex was anathema to the Calvinistic chairman. Dinosaurs weren't quite extinct.

Sandra opened the door and entered the office. 'Mrs Frayne has just rung. I offered to put her through, but she said not to bother, just to tell you she'll not be home until late.'

'Thanks.'

'I've got everything right up to date. If there's nothing urgent, do you think I could leave?'

'This early?'

She smiled winningly. 'It's Tom's birthday.'

'Your brother?'

'My boyfriend.'

'I thought you told me his name was Giles?'

'That's weeks ago.'

She had a deep, loving relationship with her boyfriend; it was he who kept changing. 'If you're sure everything's in order?'

'Couldn't be more so.'

'OK.'

He watched her leave, then leaned back in the chair and stared at the framed print on the far wall of a winter

scene in which a single-cowl oast house was the centre
of the composition. When they'd become engaged, Portia
and he had house-hunted. They'd viewed an oast house,
abutting a village green, which had epitomized much of
what he loved about the countryside. For her, it had held
no attraction because she'd recently read that converted
oast houses were for the pseudo-smarties. A month later,
they'd bought – she had bought – an Edwardian pile in
Fretstone, which she had had furnished by a professional
who, one hoped, had sufficient taste never to live in one
of his own settings.

Never marry for money, but don't scorn it if it's there.
Lousy advice for a man. No one charged a higher rate of
interest than a wealthy wife . . .

His life had been smooth and comfortable until his
parents had been killed in a plane crash. The shock of
their deaths had been compounded when it had become
obvious that far from enjoying a comfortable inheritance
– which the family lifestyle had led him to expect –
there was almost nothing left in the kitty; even the
seventeenth-century farmhouse, twenty acres of grassland,
and fifty-acre wood, were heavily mortgaged. Knowing
how much his mother had loved living on their small
estate, his father had been unable to find the courage to
warn her that his losses at Lloyd's threatened both estate
and lifestyle and instead had sought to recoup those losses
on the stock market, forgetting one of the immutable rules
of life – losers keep losing.

His plans for the future had been turned into confetti.
About to start his second year at university, he had been
unable to fund himself and had applied for a grant. That
had been denied on the grounds he had not needed one
during his first year. Equality of opportunity for all decreed
that past privilege prevented present subsidy.

Fate and bureaucracy pointed to failure, so a goddamn
failure he'd be. He'd become a drifter, had sought relief

from reality in drugs, had stolen to fund his drug taking. And he had been able to justify himself until he'd teamed up with Mick and Ken . . .

Mick had claimed that the old man who lived in the house on his own had a collection of silver that was worth a fortune; he knew a fence who'd take it all at a fair price. The old man was only half a step ahead of senility and the house was virtually wide open since all the locks were simple and there were no alarms. There couldn't be an easier mark this side of a blind man's purse. They'd stolen a car – Ken would be inside any make of car within two minutes – and driven the nine miles to the house, which stood on a slight rise from which the nearest town could be seen. They'd climbed the brick wall on the opposite side to the road and Ken had had the back door open in twenty seconds. Which was when they'd learned Mick's information left a lot to be desired. There were alarms and there was a giant Schnauzer which, at such a moment of tension, made the Hound of the Baskervilles seem like a Peke. It had taken hold of Mick and begun to chew while the alarm triggered a wailing hooter that was the Last Trump off-key. Ken and he had panicked and fled.

During the following days, he asked himself again and again, would Mick identify Ken and him to the police in exchange for promised or implied leniency; how could he have been such a bloody fool; how could he have been so weak as to think his bitterness justified his abjuring all the standards he had been brought up to observe? As the days became weeks, he had begun to hope; as the weeks became months, he understood that Mick was observing his standards and had refused to name his fellow thieves. It was Mick's silence which made him swear to himself that his drifting, drugging, and stealing days were at an end; he would prove he was man enough to face the world, full frontal.

It was, as always, a sight easier to formulate a resolution than to keep it. Lacking a degree in a world where one was the necessary passport to most jobs with a future, he had had to take whatever was on offer. He'd stacked shelves in supermarkets, failed to be hired as an assistant in a shoe shop because his accent was too 'posh' for their normal clients, even swept the streets. He'd begun to identify his resolution as pie-in-the-sky; he lay in the gutter, yet could not even look up at the stars because they had disappeared . . .

One day, he'd read in *The Times* that a distant cousin's wife had been killed in an air crash and on an impulse – irrational since he'd met the other only once, years before, and hadn't liked him, but his parents had died in similar circumstances – he'd phoned Riley to express his condolences. He'd been invited to the other's home and three weekends later had travelled there. They'd quickly discovered that the only thing they had in common was loss, but that proved sufficient for him to be invited some months later to a party to celebrate Riley's engagement to an old friend who'd been widowed.

He'd met Portia at that party. She was a little too tall, a little too thin; her features were heavy, her manner abrupt and touched with a hint of imperiousness. As they drank Heidsieck – she matched him glass for glass – he learned that she had definite, conservative opinions and resented having these challenged.

The next day, just before he was due to leave, Riley had said: 'Portia's just rung to thank me for the party. She asked who you were and where you lived. It's not like her to show an interest in anyone but herself, so I'd say you've made your mark.'

'Probably a black one.'

Riley had laughed. 'Her father's a real bind – worked his way up from nothing and wants everyone to know that – but he's well loaded and she's the only child; the mother died years ago.'

Had he really made an impression? Unlikely and meaningless. But at that time he'd been employed as a clerk in an office where the work was boring and the supervisor a woman of indeterminate age who suffered from halitosis and a sour nature. Before long, the contrast between his life and that which Riley was living, truly a life of Riley, made him wonder just how well loaded Portia's father was.

He'd asked Riley for Portia's phone number.

'Get your oar in there, old boy, and you'll not need to scull very hard.'

He'd phoned Portia's home. A woman with a broad Kentish accent had told him Miss Westley was out. He'd phoned again that evening. Portia had said that she would like to have dinner with him.

A month and several meetings later, he'd looked in the mirror and tried to see an honest reflection. He wasn't in love with her, but he gained the impression that she was with him. It was a modern concept that one should marry for love; in past times, it had been the way of consolidating possessions. Far more realistic since if love could bloom, it must also fade, but possessions remained. The only problem, he had no possessions . . .

Nothing ventured, possibility lost. He'd proposed and she had accepted without showing the slightest interest in his financial present and future. That should have alerted him, but didn't. Only after marriage did he understand that what she had been seeking was the end of spinsterhood when friends were married, a husband whose social manners would never betray her background as did her father's, and the dominance which wealth gave those who possessed it over those who did not.

Westley had had so many fingers in so many pies that his nickname had been Four-arm Cyril. He'd had a word with an acquaintance – he'd been too successful to have friends – and Andrew & Sachs had offered him – Frayne – a job without bothering about an interview to determine whether he had any experience.

Westley had died suddenly, less than a year after their marriage. When the estate had finally been sorted out, she had become a wealthy woman. Her manner towards others as well as him had become more autocratic and before long she had suggested, i.e. demanded, he move into one of the other bedrooms so that she could sleep better . . .

A nearby church clock struck the half-hour and brought him back to the present. He looked down at the top folder on the desk. To his surprise, and probably that of many others, he had a talent for the work. His present pilot would be warmly welcomed by the commissioning clients if it were presented to them – which it possibly wouldn't be because the chairman would veto its submission, deeming the matter offensive even though a professional Mrs Grundy would find nothing to object to.

He opened a second folder and returned to work. At seven, he returned papers to the folder, rubbed his eyes, yawned. That Portia, who ordered her life carefully, had suddenly decided to be out that evening meant something unexpected had happened. Had Winifred had a row with her sister – which seemed to happen every visit – and returned home two days early? Portia had become friendly with Winifred after her father had died; shortly before she had decided they should sleep in different bedrooms.

He stood, did not move immediately as he tried to decide what to do. He'd play it straight, he decided. Unlike Oscar, he could resist temptation.

He went downstairs and left the building by the back door, making certain he double-locked it, crossed to his Audi which now was the only car left in the small, private car park. He settled behind the wheel, inserted the key, but did not turn it. He brought the mobile out of his pocket and dialled home. The phone rang several times, then clicked into message mode. He had not expected Portia to be home and it was now confirmed that she was not. But what did that matter, he tried to ask himself, if he'd decided to drive straight home?

At the end of the high street, the lights were at red. He braked to a halt. Crossroads, he thought fancifully, reflected life – depending on which way one turned, one reached a different destination. Continue straight on and he would arrive at Bell's House, a monument to smart chic and as welcoming as an empty igloo; turn left and in twenty minutes' time he would be at Thoburn Cottage, the epitome of casual comfort, more welcoming than the antechamber to Shangri-La . . . Not that these crossroads were offering him an alternative since he had made his decision not to turn. When the lights changed, he turned left.

East Fretstone had been developed between the wars and the roads were lined with detached houses in their own grounds and semi-detached ones with small front and larger back gardens. If the south was the smart part of town, the east offered the best value for money. He passed a small shopping area – noted for the independent baker whose bread tasted as all bread had once tasted – and more houses and then abruptly was in the countryside. Green fields, thorn hedges, copses, grazing animals, timber-framed houses, barns . . . Sometimes he found it difficult to believe that once he had enjoyed all those things. Had Laycock Farm altered since the death of his parents? He hoped not. A seventeenth-century house with its small rooms and low ceilings might suffer certain disadvantages, but to try to eradicate these by adding to the structure was to lessen the history.

He passed the small ragstone church in which Francesca had been married. She'd told him that the vicar, an old man who should have retired years before, had called her Francis when asking her whether she would take William to be her lawfully wedded husband. 'I didn't realize it was such a bad omen.' He'd known the pain of someone else's despair when she'd said that.

The lane, bordered on both sides by overgrown hedges which contained so many varieties of plants they could be dated as centuries old, twisted and turned as if the shortest distance between two points was a spiral. He passed Hangman's Cross, which was proudly reputed to have been the site of gallows (a fact never authenticated), and reached the hamlet of Larnhurst. Straight over, turn left, past half a dozen bungalows which had been built decades before when planing permission had not been needed, and turn right into the drive of Thoburn Cottage. It was small, ragstone and brick to the first floor level, then clapboard to the eaves, with a peg-tile roof. As country properties went, it was ordinary, but he would have swapped Portia's Edwardian mansion for it any day of the week.

He parked by the side of the shed, used as a garage, which was reputedly a World War I army hut. The state of the corrugated iron roof and wooden sides made it obvious that Francesca could not afford to have repairs carried out.

He opened the straked wooden gate, showing initial signs of rot where the paint had flaked away, and went along the brick path and around the corner of the house. The garden was small, full of colour, and free of weeds despite the intractable nature of the heavy clay soil; Francesca said that gardening provided some of her few moments of mental peace. Beyond the garden was a field which dipped away to a small bourne, beyond which were woods. He heard the call of a disturbed cock pheasant. He'd shot his first pheasant on a neighbour's land and his father had not been told it had been poached until after it was eaten. 'When the mind's not told, the stomach doesn't go hungry,' his mother had said, recognizing her husband's strict adherence to the country's sporting code.

He opened the outer door of the small porch as Francesca

opened the inner one. 'I didn't expect you here,' she said sharply.

'I didn't expect to be here.'

She hesitated, then moved to one side.

He entered the hall, triangular shaped because the long, sharply sloping roof formed an outshut. 'I was heading for home, but the car insisted on turning instead of going straight on at the crossroads.'

'Really!'

'German cars don't like taking orders from British drivers.' He often spoke nonsense to her; it was one way of suppressing emotion. Her face was lined and her expression one of dull acceptance. If only, he thought. 'How's Bill?'

'Yesterday, he kept asking when he could come home. It's the terrible up and down, never knowing—' She stopped abruptly.

He wanted to hug and comfort her, reminding her there was happiness as well as tragedy, but knew that however much she might long for this assurance, she would refuse to receive it from him. 'Can't the doctor do something more to help?'

'It doesn't seem so. He's said there'll be remissions, but I mustn't expect these to last; Bill can continue as he is for years. But I don't think I can take much more . . . Hell! Come on through and have a drink and talk about something cheerful.'

She had black, curly hair, wide apart deep-blue eyes that expressed more than she sometimes wished, a retroussé nose, a full mouth that could, but these days seldom did, laugh so warmly that even a misogynist would smile back, a slim body that did all the right things in the right places, and long, slender hands with which she often gesticulated with southern European enthusiasm, an echo of her maternal Spanish grandmother.

He followed her into the beamed sitting room, which

had a large inglenook fireplace. She came to a stop in the middle, the central beam only two inches above her head. 'I can only offer gin or beer. I haven't had time to replenish stocks.'

Or the money, he thought. The cost of the nursing home in which her husband lived, partly in this world, partly in another, was rapidly depleting her financial resources. 'A gin and tonic would go down a treat.'

She crossed to the small cocktail trolley, to the side of the single window, and as she pulled apart the two halves of the top, a shelf with holders for bottles and glasses rose. 'Would you like some ice?'

'I'll get it.' He went into the hall and through to the kitchen. Dirty plates and cutlery were stacked up on one of the draining boards. Her depression had to be unusually severe since normally she was a tidy person. He dropped half a dozen ice cubes into a cup, carried this back to the sitting room. As he watched her pouring the drinks, he found himself visualizing the flesh beneath the print dress.

She handed him a glass, sat. 'I'm glad you came,' she said abruptly

'I'm glad to hear you're glad! To tell the truth, I rather gathered from your greeting that you might have preferred a visit from the tax inspector.'

'I'm sorry.'

'For Heaven's sake, you'd every cause to tell me to b. off.'

'It's just . . . you know how it goes.'

He probably did. She welcomed his company even while she thought of herself as a traitor to Bill because she did.

She stared with unfocused eyes at the fireplace and the firebasket, in which she'd set a bowl of red and yellow roses. 'Sometimes . . .'

'Tell me.'

She shook her head.

'It might help to say it.'

She fidgeted with a curl that looped down over her forehead. 'Sometimes I become so down, I'm certain I can't carry on.'

'Give yourself a break; go away for a few days.'

'I can't.'

'Why not?'

'He gets so agitated if he doesn't see me every day.'

'Better he misses you than that you break down.'

'I won't do that,' she said firmly, forgetting that only a moment ago she had doubted her ability to continue.

Life could be so much crueller than death, he thought.

She drank. 'Goddamnit, I said to come in here to talk about something cheerful and here we are, glooming away . . . How's Portia?'

'That's a cheerful subject?'

'I wish you wouldn't say things like that.'

'Humble apologies.'

'Which aren't in the least bit humble . . . I met Lisa the other day and she asked after you.'

'Lisa?'

'You don't remember her? She would be pleased if I told her that! She thinks you're rather a handsome dish.'

'A discerning woman.'

'If you could remember her, you'd know she's one of the most undiscerning women you'll ever meet.' She smiled briefly.

If they were together, he'd make her smile or laugh much of the time.

He had put down the paperback, turned off the light, and settled down in the bed when he heard a car drive into the courtyard so quickly that Portia had to brake fiercely enough to make the brakes squeal. Recently, he'd suggested it would be a good idea when she visited

Winifred to stay the night. His suggestion had infuriated her. Was that because the inference was she drank to excess or that she would willingly wish to spend the night there?

A door was slammed shut. She often used doors as a means of expressing emotion. Anger caused by frustration?

Three

L ynch stared through the open doorway of the hut at the heavy rain which reduced visibility to feet. If it continued at the same intensity, the plan had to be at risk . . . The stench of rotting vegetation seemed to increase and he brought from his right-hand trouser pocket the silk handkerchief he had doused with his favourite perfume before leaving the hotel. He put it to his nose.

Somewhere out in the rain, Togba and the eleven others were waiting and watching. That was, if they weren't huddled together in some shelter and not even in sight of the river. He'd repeatedly tried to impress on Togba that success depended on surprise, which was why his plan must be carried out as laid down; repeatedly, Togba had answered: 'Everything good, boss. No worry. Togba very smart.'

The rain eased and then stopped within the space of five minutes. A good omen. He heard a harsh, tuneless bird call which rose in volume, then was abruptly cut off. Had it been given by a real bird or was it Togba's warning that the boat had been sighted? Togba had earlier sounded the call so that he could recognize it, but hadn't explained how to distinguish the false from the true, being too busy explaining that the bird was so popular because those who ate it were able to enjoy very good bong-bong . . .

The call was repeated and a troop of monkeys began to chatter. The boat was coming.

He stood. He would have liked to make certain he

would not be at risk, but judged Dijkstal viewed him with sufficient contempt to be convinced that he would never knowingly be within reach of danger so his presence would negate the possibility there could be any.

He crossed to the doorway. Only Togba and the one-eyed man who owned the boat which had brought them up the river were visible. So far, so good. He left the hut and began to walk across land so sodden that at each step water welled up over his shoes. This exacerbated his discomfort.

He reached the tumbledown landing stage. The boat had not yet rounded the bend in the river. He stared at the water, dreading the ripple that would herald an approaching snake . . . A long, narrow boat, similar to the one he had arrived in, rounded the bend and approached the landing stage. He counted. Dijkstal and six armed men, the same number as before. He was surprised, having expected Dijkstal, since he would have a fortune in diamonds on him, to have brought at least a couple more bodyguards . . . Another craft appeared and in this were six armed men.

'Many,' said Togba, making Lynch start because he'd not seen the other approach. 'But they from east. Women!'

A gun in the hands of a woman was just as lethal as in the hands of a man. His mind raced. Because the landing stage was usable for only part of its length, both boats could not tie up and the men disembark at the same time. If those ashore had sufficient intelligence to realize the plan had to be altered . . .

'Hullo, there,' Dijkstal called out as the bows of the leading boat turned inshore.

'Good afternoon,' he called back, conscious his voice was strained. Like a bloody social meeting. Soon, the cucumber sandwiches would appear . . .

The approaching boat's bows began to fall off because the current was stronger than the helmsman had judged and he briefly gunned the outboard to gain more way. Dijkstal shouted at him, annoyed their arrival should be marked by incompetent handling. The second helmsman throttled back until the boat, in relation to the bank, was stationary.

The first boat came alongside. Three men stepped on to the landing stage, rifles held negligently because they could perceive no cause for alarm. Dijkstal eased his way past them and, hand outstretched, greeted Lynch. 'Great to see you again, Esme.' He shook hands enthusiastically.

One of the remaining armed men in the boat climbed onto the landing stage. The second boat began to turn.

'You're looking a bit peaky,' Dijkstal observed.

'I've had a go of gippy tummy,' Lynch replied hurriedly.

'Have you been eating unskinned fruit? First rule of the tropics. Never touch anything unless you can peel it.'

A second man climbed out of the boat, but could not move forward because the rest of the group were held back as Lynch had not moved. The third and last man remained standing in the boat.

'Where's your companion?' Dijkstal asked.

'The man who drove the boat is . . .'

'My dear Esme, a man pilots or sails, he does not drive a boat . . . I meant, the man who knows all there is to know about diamonds?' His tone was ironic.

Lynch had forgotten that he had said he would be bringing along an expert to value the diamonds. 'He's in the hut.'

'He is of a retiring nature?'

'Very much so, because he has a worse case of tummy than me.'

'Small wonder the newcomers are called gallopers . . . Tell me, have you remembered the usquebaugh?'

'The what?'

'Is that not the true name for whisky?'

'Oh! Of course. I found some Haig in a store near the hotel.'

'So you have not been vague!' Dijkstal laughed. 'Now tell me, how many bottles have you brought?'

'Six.'

'You have unlocked the gates of paradise. And if there are also a few cigarettes . . . ?'

'A carton of Chesterfields.'

'Then you have opened them wide. Now, let us do business together so that soon we can toast success.'

Lynch did not move. Every second gained could be valuable since the hidden men had – he hoped to hell they realized this – to take up new positions. 'You have the telephone number of your bank?'

'Of course. Time is of the essence if I am to make a safe place before dark after leaving here, so please let us move.'

His tone had become sharp, Lynch thought. Had he sensed danger, yet was unable to see where it might lie? The armed men remained bunched; the second boat was almost alongside and the occupants were momentarily more interested in an argument between two of them than in what was happening ashore. 'It shouldn't be long before you leave us,' he said. When he saw the change in Dijkstal's expression, he realized he'd reinforced the other's suspicions by what he'd just said and he cursed his warped sense of humour. He turned and walked to the end of the landing stage and onto the land. He took a step forward, appeared to trip and fall, lay spreadeagled on the sodden land.

The sound of many Kalashnikovs firing off their thirty-round magazines in full automatic mode hurt the eardrums. Dijkstal, thrown backwards, was dead before he hit the ground; the six on the landing stage collapsed and four fell into the water, the six in the boat who had not been the primary targets had time to respond and raise their rifles, but only two began to fire before they, and the helmsman, were cut down. The boat, the outboard in neutral, was caught by the current and brought into the bank. Two men stood up and emptied their magazines into the huddle of bodies.

Lynch came to his feet.

'You swim?' Togba sniggered.

Lynch, embarrassed, hoped the other thought the only cause of his sodden clothing was the wet vegetation and soil. 'Make the two boats fast.'

'OK, boss.'

As Togba gave orders to the men, who were boasting about how many each had slaughtered, Lynch crossed to where Dijkstal lay, on his back, arms outstretched, one leg under him, one out at an angle, shirt punctured and bloody, part of his jaw missing and one eye socket a gruesome mess. Lynch struggled to prevent himself causing contemptuous amusement by vomiting. Blood scared him and wounds aroused overwhelming disgust, but he leaned over the dead and shattered man and searched him. There were two black velvet bags and in the first were several stones, in the second, a single one. He rolled the single diamond in the palm of his hand. He was no gemmologist, but knew more about diamonds than he had admitted. It was his tentative judgement that in truth Dijkstal had been conservative in his estimation of the value of that stone.

Lynch poured himself a very large whisky, added bottled water, and wished he dared add ice without risking a host of waterborne diseases.

'What about me?' Drury, sprawled across the settee, demanded roughly.

Lynch hesitated. But since there was small point in antagonizing the other – fifteen stone of bone and muscle and an argumentative nature – he poured out a second whisky.

'I'll have it straight.'

'Then come and get it.'

Drury stood, crossed the floor.

'Keep off the booze while you're with her,' Lynch said, as he passed the glass across.

'You think you need to tell me my job?'

'As I always say, there's no harm in making certain two people are speaking the same language.'

'So tell me what one you speak?'

Lynch wasn't certain what implication lay behind those words.

As Drury sat once more on the settee, Carol entered. She came to a stop and stared curiously at him.

'Let me introduce you to Reg,' Lynch said.

She said hullo, Drury nodded. Each immediately identified the other for what he or she was.

'Do I get a drink?' she asked.

'Help yourself,' Lynch replied.

She poured out a whisky, added water from the bottle.

'I'll be leaving soon,' Lynch said. 'You'll stay until tomorrow and then return with Reg.'

She turned round, glass in her right hand. 'Why's he going to be with me?'

'To escort you back and see there aren't any problems at the flat.'

'Escort, my arse. You mean guard.'

'Escorting sounds much nicer.'

'What flat?'

'All will be revealed in good time.'

She drank. 'There wasn't nothing said about being in a flat.'

'Then treat the news as a pleasant surprise.'

'Pleasant?'

'It is to be hoped so.'

'I don't like it. Suppose I say I ain't going to no flat?'

'I'm sure you don't want to be found with your throat cut in one of the less salubrious gutters in this stinking town.'

Brief fear tightened her face. She crossed to a chair and sat.

Drury brought a pack of cigarettes out of his pocket.

'Not in here,' Lynch said. 'The smell of cigarette smoke distresses me.'

Drury replaced the pack in his pocket. He looked at Carol and wondered if she'd be able to teach him anything he didn't already know when they were in the flat.

The immigration officer opened Lynch's passport, thumbed through the pages, looked up at him, then back down at the passport. He tapped several keys of the computer terminal, studied the small VDU. 'Mr Esme Lynch?'

'So I have always understood,' Lynch jovially replied.

'And you've just returned from Sierra Leone?'

'That's right.'

The immigration officer picked up a telephone receiver and spoke briefly in a low voice. Behind Lynch, waiting passengers began to voice annoyance at the delay.

A customs officer, three gold bars on his uniform, came across to the desk. The seated immigration officer handed him the passport. 'Mr Esme Lynch?'

'That is I.'

'And you've just returned from Sierra Leone?'

'How many more times do you have to ask the same questions?' demanded the man with a ginger moustache who stood immediately behind Lynch.

'As many times as we deem necessary. And that applies to every incoming passenger.'

The man accepted it was in his interest to suffer the delay quietly.

'Would you be kind enough to accompany me?' the customs officer asked.

'Do I have an option?' Lynch asked.

He smiled.

Lynch was directed to a small room, barely furnished and

with blue-tinged overhead lights that possessed a quality which made the fittest complexion look as if it was borne by a consumptive.

'Please sit down.'

As he sat, a second and younger man, with one gold bar, came into the room. He and his companion sat on the opposite side of the stained, scarred wooden table that was set squarely under the lights.

Lynch was asked why he had visited Sierra Leone. He wondered why they were interested in his reason. It was their job, the younger man replied, to be interested in why certain people visited certain places and he was one of those persons and Sierra Leone was one of those places.

'I decided I needed a holiday.'

'Funny sort of place to have a holiday.'

'It makes a change from Magaluf.'

'Anywhere would do that. Have you in your possession anything obtained in Sierra Leone, either by gift or purchase?'

'All I've come back with that I didn't have when I left is a tummy bug.'

'You don't have any drugs?'

'Of course not.'

'What about diamonds?'

'Do I look like a diamond dealer?'

'There's no standard appearance for such people,' said the elder officer, speaking with pompous seriousness. 'Do you have anything illegal in your luggage?'

'I've just answered.'

'You will have no objection to our searching it?'

'No . . . You've just reminded me. My two cases will be going round and round on the carousel.'

'They have been retrieved.'

The cases were brought into the room and searched so thoroughly that a stowaway mosquito would have been exposed. They asked him if he would object to a body search.

'I most certainly would. I mean, having to strip off in front of two strangers!'

'Surely you welcome the idea?' said the younger officer and was immediately rebuked by his senior.

When the body search had been completed and Lynch had checked the knot of his silk tie in the cracked mirror, he expressed with some force the sense of mortification the search had occasioned him. The elder officer listened politely for a while, then interrupted to ask if Lynch would object to being X-rayed. If he did – perhaps on medical grounds – he would have to stay in a special unit until nature had taken its course and confirmed that he had not attempted to smuggle something by swallowing it just before leaving Sierra Leone. He agreed to an X-ray and was driven to a nearby hospital.

Later, after having received a negative report on the X-ray, the elder officer thanked Lynch for his cooperation. The younger officer made another comment that earned him a rebuke.

Four hours after he had arrived at the airport, Lynch left it in a taxi. He was grateful that the driver was a loquacious man. The endless, inane chatter helped to keep memories at bay; a man of taste, he found the mental image of Dijkstal's head after part of the jaw and one eye had been blown away very distressing.

Four

Throughout the flight, as they passed immigration, and as they collected their luggage from the carousel, an interested onlooker would have seen nothing to suggest that Drury and Carol knew each other. Only when they were in the main hall, assured of anonymity by the endless hubbub of people, did he speak to her.

As she walked, having to move her legs far more quickly than he to keep close to him, she cursed herself for being so complete a fool as to become mixed up in something that really scared her. Hadn't she learned too much . . . ?

He stopped in front of a message board, scanned the contents, picked out an envelope. They continued to the end of the hall and left through a doorway that led to the car parks. He came to a stop, slit open the envelope and from it brought a car key, a sheet of paper, and a parking card. He read what was written, resumed walking without speaking to her.

Her growing fear – fuelled by imagination – might have panicked her into breaking away had Lynch not made it cruelly clear that any attempt to do so would ensure Norma suffered.

Drury ignored the lifts and walked up the sloping ramps to the second floor, paid the parking fee, then continued through to the west end and a green Vauxhall Astra parked in the second row from the outside. He activated the remote unlocking, opened the boot and put in it the suitcase he had been carrying, motioned to her to do the same with hers, slammed the lid shut. He settled behind the wheel and started the engine before she was seated.

'Where are we going?' she asked.

'You'll find out when we get there.' He backed out and turned.

'Why won't you say now?'

'Because it's me orders not to,' he answered as they began to spiral down to ground level.

She remained silent until they had passed through the barrier and were on the road. 'How long am I going to have to stay wherever we're going?'

'Ain't that obvious?' He sounded genuinely surprised she should need to ask. 'There ain't no need to worry. You want a drink, some decent grub instead of the muck we've been having to eat, you'll get it. I'll see to that.'

She did not need to wonder what was activating this newly displayed friendliness. Men differed, their desires didn't.

They turned on to the motorway. 'Have you worked for the fat git before?' he suddenly asked.

'No.'

'Me neither . . . The way he ponces around, Esme's the right name. Only he can't be no fool, the racket he's running. You've got to hand him that.'

Ahead, a car suddenly changed lanes without giving any signal, forcing Drury to brake. He shouted threats at the other driver. Given the opportunity, she thought, he'd carry out those threats with careless efficiency. She must do or say nothing to arouse his quick temper. Which shouldn't be difficult, since it was her job to keep men happy.

'I've been thinking,' he said.

Experience suggested that provided he didn't think she was scornfully laughing at him, he would appreciate being twitted; he'd imagine she was warming to him. 'Don't overdo things.'

He put his left hand on her right knee. 'You and me can have a good time together.'

'Doing what?'

'It won't be the crossword.' He chuckled as he slid his hand halfway up her thigh. 'You're solo, ain't you?'

'No.' The bastard knew she had a daughter. 'I've a kid.'

'Wouldn't have thought you was old enough.'

Every man a comic.

'So we'll take her with us.'

'Where to?'

'A cruise on the square rigger what's just . . .' He became silent.

She tried to gain a more comfortable position and he moved his hand higher.

'Biggest ever built. Does cruises and sails across the Atlantic. Always wanted to do that – sail across the Atlantic in a square rigger. Stand out on deck and see all those sails, hear the rigging strumming, feel the wheel kicking in your hands . . . You'd like that.'

'Not if it kicked too high.'

He chuckled, slid his hand further up. 'I guess your kid would be real excited?'

'Can't say.'

'I like kids.'

That seemed about as likely as a punter with a heart of gold. Did he imagine that if he said he liked kids, she'd welcome him instead of suffering him? Hypocrisy was every man's middle name. Always trying to make out it was affection, not lust, which drove him to humiliate a woman.

He edged the Astra into the inside lane, after two hundred yards drove off the motorway onto the slip road.

'Are we near the flat?' she asked.

'It ain't far to go.'

She looked through the side window at the fields and the scatter of houses. Her dream was to live somewhere where her past was left behind and Norma could grow up in clean, healthy surroundings and not wonder how her mother made her money. Like so many dreams, hers was corny and naive. Unless Norma could somehow escape the world she lived in now, her chance of enjoying a better life than her mother's was too close to nil to call.

'What you thinking?' he asked.

'That I'd like to live somewhere like around here.'

'So what would you do for kicks – talk to the bleeding cows?'

'What would you do on the square rigger – talk to the bleeding sails?'

That amused him. He returned his hand to her thigh. 'You've a quick tongue.'

'There's been some who haven't complained.'

'I'll guess.' He moved his hand higher.

'How much longer is it?'

'Longer than a moment back.'

'I meant, the journey.'

Due to his inattention, the car had drifted too close to the verge and he had to release her thigh and put both hands on the wheel to correct their course. When they were driving more safely, he returned his left hand.

'Can't you wait?' she asked.

'Don't you like a bit of pleasure?'

Pleasure? Did he think he was making her day for her? 'If we end up in the ditch, there won't be much pleasure around.'

'I could drive one-handed to Scotland.' To add emphasis to his words, he raised his hand still higher.

She was a nervous passenger and when she judged they were in danger of colliding with a sign post, she drew in her breath with an audible hiss.

'Me too,' he said, as he put on sufficient lock to avoid a collision. 'So we'll do something about it.'

They reached a wooded area and along this was a natural layby into which he drove.

Fifteen minutes later, as the light was fading, he started the engine and drew out. They had gone several hundred yards when the car lurched and swerved. He sawed at the wheel, trying to regain control, but put on too much lock and the rear end skidded to swing the front end around and send the nearside up onto the grass verge, yet not so abruptly that the airbags were activated.

'What happened?' she asked shrilly.

'A puncture,' he answered, larding his words with many adjectives. 'Picked up something when we parked.'

She hoped that didn't apply to her as well.

Still swearing, he opened the driver's door, climbed out, and checked the front tyres. He kicked the nearside one.

She lowered her window. 'Is it a puncture?'

His answer was to kick the tyre a second time. 'Come here,' he shouted.

She opened her door and because of the angle at which the car had come to a stop, stepped out onto the grass verge. Her shoes sank into the soft earth. It was her turn to swear. The shoes were new, bought for the trip to Sierra Leone, and she had paid more for them than she could afford. They were smart, but not solid, and damp mud might well ruin them. She took the longest steps she could to reach the road and was about to examine her shoes when he again shouted at her. She began to walk around the Astra. As she did so, an oncoming car cleared the bend ahead on its wrong side. She realized that, because she was well out in the road, it would hit her unless she moved immediately, but it was this knowledge which left her incapable of doing anything. It struck her and hurled her against the Astra.

Five

Frayne heard the car drive into the courtyard and looked up from the television at the carriage clock on the marble mantelpiece. A quarter past ten. A door slammed; something was knocked over in the hall, but he couldn't identify what from the sound. Portia entered the blue room – as she was pleased to call the smaller drawing room – and crossed unsteadily to the nearest armchair, into which she collapsed rather than sat. 'Do you have to have the sound so loud?' she demanded, her pronunciation fuzzy.

It wasn't loud. He switched off the television with the remote control. She disliked nature films on the grounds that they were boring. He thought it more likely that her dislike arose from the fact that animals were no respecters of social conventions.

'I want a drink.'

'You don't think . . .' he began.

'No, I bloody well don't.'

Swearing, she maintained, was a sign of lack of breeding. He stood. 'What would you like?'

'The usual.'

He noticed that her hands were trembling. Her expression was strained. 'Is something wrong?'

'Of course it isn't.'

'But you're shaking.'

'Because I'm cold.'

A less than convincing explanation. The day had been hot and the night was pleasantly warm. 'Are you sure nothing's happened?'

'Yes.'

He left the room, crossed the hall, and went down a short stretch of passage to the small room which had originally been the butler's pantry. Bottles were kept in the cupboard with solid doors, glasses in the one with glass doors. He poured into a silver cocktail shaker a measure of tequila, one of Cointreau, a spoonful of sugar, the juice of a lime, and two cubes of ice taken from the refrigerator by the side of the small marble-surrounded sink, shook vigorously, poured the contents into a glass. He gave himself a more quickly produced gin and tonic.

She seemed to have fallen asleep during his absence, to judge from the way she jerked up her head as he entered. When she took the glass, her hand was shaking so much that some of the liquid spilled over the rim.

'Do you think you've got a fever?'

'Can't you understand, I'm all right?' she demanded violently. She drank quickly.

He sat. That something had disturbed her was obvious. She hadn't said she'd been at Winifred's – she seldom did – but if she had and had drunk too generously, then perhaps she had upset Winifred when the alcohol exacerbated her imperious, snobby manner and there had been a row. Her relationship with Winifred seemed to be on a considerably higher emotional plane than hers with him.

She drained her glass. 'I want another.'

'D'you think that's wise?'

'Don't start trying to tell me what I can and can't do . . . Who pays for everything?'

'In the interests of accuracy, I settle the bills for drinks.'

'With my money.'

'With the money I earn by the sweat of my brow.'

'I pay Ethel more than you earn.'

'She'd be very surprised to hear that. And incidentally, her name's Enid.'

'Always have to argue, don't you?'

'That's the downside of being right.'

'You think you're so smart!' She picked up her glass and tried to drink from it, realized it was empty. 'Are you going to get me another or do I have to do it?'

Normally, she tried – even where he was concerned – to conceal her sour nature under a cloak of reasonable, if superior, affability, and that made her present open antagonism as unusual as was the fact that she was not trying to hide her heavy drinking. He picked up the glass from the occasional table at the side of her chair and returned to the butler's pantry. If the cause of her ill-tempered drunkenness had been a row, it must have been a very bitter one. He squeezed the juice from a lime. Bitter enough to mark the end of the friendship? Too much to hope for.

She drank the second margarita as quickly as she had the first. 'I'm going to bed,' she said, as she put the glass down heavily on the table.

'I hope you sleep well,' he replied, rather more ironically than intended.

She stood, had hurriedly to grab the back of the chair for support. He stood, showing old-fashioned manners. She crossed the room, every step calling for concentration, and opened the door, forgetting it swung inwards. It struck her shoulder and she almost fell. He hurried over and took hold of her left arm to support her.

'You're not coming into my bedroom!' She shrugged herself free.

'I assure you my concerns were of a different physical nature.'

She left. He stood in the doorway and watched her take a circuitous route across the hall to the stairs. The heavy mahogany balustrade provided sufficient support for her to climb up with a degree of certainty and a small measure of dignity.

When she reached the landing and turned right to go out

of sight, he returned to his chair, sat, and finished his drink. Marriage was like a lottery – there were very many more losers than winners.

The paramedic crossed the road to the police car which was parked twenty yards from the nearest flashing warning light, set out because it would soon be dark. 'We're off, then.'

'What's the verdict?'

'Not a chance. Her skull must be like a jigsaw.' He returned to the ambulance, which drove off.

Swift drew back the sleeve of his uniform jacket and noted the time, wrote that down together with the words, *Ambulance left scene with victim aboard.* He pocketed the notebook, went over to where a few onlookers were standing. 'Can any of you tell me anything about the accident?' There was silence. 'How about you?' he said to the young man nearest to him.

'Not me.'

'Then why don't you carry on?'

'Only wanted to see if I could give a hand.'

And the superintendent of B division was a kind, thoughtful superior. 'Thanks, mate,' he said, as if he meant that, 'but there's nothing to do.'

The man walked back to where he'd left his car; his departure signalled a general movement and soon only an elderly man remained.

'There's nothing for you to do, Dad,' Swift said, not hiding his annoyance.

'I thought you was asking if anyone see anything?'

His manner changed. 'If you did, I'd be grateful to hear what that was.'

'I saw her being hit. Like she was a rag doll. 'Orrible. It's us what rung nine, nine, nine.'

'Where were you when you saw the accident?'

'In me garden.' He pointed.

Four to five hundred yards along the road, and now marked by a lighted window, was a cottage. 'I'd like to hear more, but I've things to do first. Suppose you return home and I'll be with you as soon as possible.'

Swift crossed to the police car and used the radio to call HQ and ask if a recovery vehicle was on its way. He was assured it was.

For the next fifteen minutes, with the aid of a torch, he checked car, road, and roadside, and made certain the sketched details of the scene were as accurate as possible.

A low-loader arrived and the Astra was winched onto it. As it drove off, he noted down the time. He collected up the two warning lights and put them in the boot of the police car, noted the time. Bureaucratic rules demanded that every i was dotted twice and every t crossed thrice and if that took up time which could have been more productively spent elsewhere, so be it. Priorities had to be observed.

A car, travelling very quickly, approached; when its headlights picked out the marked police car, the driver slowed right down and passed Swift at so reasonable a speed he had to brake only briefly for the corner.

He lit a cigarette. The only person in the Astra – a youngish woman who might have been attractive before the accident – had, after the puncture which presumably had caused the car to swerve, been walking around it. An oncoming vehicle had rounded the corner well on its wrong side, failed to correct its position, hit her and slammed her head against the window. Daytime measurements would confirm, but his estimate was that when the driver first could sight the stationary Astra, there should have been sufficient distance for him to slow and pull right over onto his side of the road. That he had not done so suggested he'd been under the influence of drink or drugs, a possibility that to some degree was confirmed by his not stopping.

He dropped the cigarette butt onto the road. An initial

task was to determine the victim's identity, but for the moment that was impossible. There were no personal or car papers and no handbag. Which seemed odd. Did a woman ever leave home without a handbag? He shrugged his shoulders. One had only to declare something invariably happened to be proved wrong by its not happening. Anyway, identity could be determined by establishing in whose name the Astra was registered.

He settled behind the wheel of the police car, started the engine and drove the short distance to the cottage. As he walked up the gravel path, between flower beds that were partially illuminated by the light from the window, the front door opened.

'Come on in, then.'

He stepped into a small hall which was overburdened by a grandfather clock with a painted face. 'Sorry to bother you when it's getting late, but it's necessary. My name's PC Swift and yours is . . . ?'

'Maddock.'

The other was older than he had judged when seeing him in the growing darkness; spiky grey hair, a round face, beady eyes, and a button nose made Swift think of a cartoon character who, initially, he could not name.

'Best come through.'

He followed the other into the front room.

'It's the copper, Ma,' Maddock said.

'So I see,' she answered good-humouredly from the settee.

'Evening, Mrs Maddock,' Swift said.

She finished a row of knitting, put needles and wool down, stood. 'You'd no doubt like a cup of tea?'

'I certainly would.'

'Turn the telly off, Dad, you don't want to watch that.'

Maddock's expression, as he worked the remote control, suggested that he did. She left the room.

Swift sat, brought his notebook out of his coat pocket.

'Tell me what you saw. And try to remember everything, so take your time.' He produced a pen, pressed one end to release the ball point.

Maddock's voice was high-pitched and his speech was marked by the occasional use of a dialect word which had all but disappeared even locally. He'd been weeding one of the flower beds in the front of the garden – Ma liked her flowers. He'd been standing up, easing his back – gave a nasty twinge now and then, wasn't as young as he'd used to be – and a car went past and he'd watched it. Why? No reason, least not as he could remember. It had suddenly swerved and then kind of spun to end up on the verge. A man had climbed out and looked . . .

'There was a man as well as the woman in the car?'

'That's what I'm saying, ain't it?'

'Are you sure?'

'I saw him, didn't I? Went off into the field, he did . . .'

If Old Pullin had seen him, there'd have been some shouting, right enough! Old Pullin swore that while he drew breath, there'd be no right to roam on his land, whatever the government said . . .

Swift brought the conversation back to the matter in hand. 'Tell me what the woman did.'

'After she got out of the car, she started walking round it. Then this other comes along and hits her. Like a rag doll. I knew she was deaded.'

'Was the oncoming car travelling quickly?'

'They don't think of anyone else. And it was all over the road.'

'How d'you mean?'

'Came round the wrong side and swerving this way and that. Thought there must be something wrong with it.'

'Did it slow or briefly stop after the woman was hit?'

'If you was to ask me, I'd say it went even faster. It were doing a hundred when it went past here; hundred and twenty, more like.'

'Did you try to read the registration number?'

'Course I did.'

'D'you have any luck?'

'My eyesight ain't as good as it used to be and it were going so fast.'

'You weren't able to get any of the letters or numbers?'

'Only the first one.'

'What was that?' Swift patiently asked.

'X.'

'Could you see the driver?'

'Not really.'

'Was it a man or a woman?'

'Couldn't rightly say.'

'What was the colour of the car?'

'Silver.'

'And the make?'

'Same as the squire's.' He carefully explained that the squire wasn't really a squire, he just lived in the big house. Things weren't as they had been when he'd been a lad, more was the pity . . .

'What kind of car does the squire own?'

'Can't say. But it's big. And fast. He drives it like there ain't no one else on the road.'

Mrs Maddock returned with a tin tray on which were mugs, sugar, milk, teaspoons, a teapot with a knitted cover in the pattern of a house, and a plateful of chocolate digestive biscuits.

After eating one biscuit and then another, Swift returned to the questioning. What had happened after the car had passed the house? Maddock had shouted to Ma to phone 999 and say there'd been an accident and a woman was lying on the road.

'That's right,' she confirmed.

'Tell me more about the man,' Swift said.

There wasn't really anything more to say. He'd leaned over the woman for a short time, had gone round to the back of the car, had some trouble in picking up things in both hands, and finally made his way into and across Old Pullin's field. If Old Pullin had been there with a gun, he'd have put a load of buckshot into the trespasser's bum . . .

'Then for his sake, it's as well he wasn't there with a gun,' Swift said. He read what he'd written and mentally checked he'd covered everything.

Six

Frayne carried his breakfast on a tray through to the morning room. Left to himself, he would have eaten in the small alcove in the kitchen which the previous owner had had built, but Portia believed that only those with kitchen tastes ever ate in a kitchen.

He set out on the table small and large plates, mug of coffee, knife, fork, and teaspoon, toast rack, butter, cherry jam and marmalade, sat. Fried egg and bacon made a cheerful start to a day, even when one was faced by a directors' get-together later on.

Portia entered as he was buttering his second piece of toast. He stood and wished her a good morning.

She gave no response, sat.

She looked really jaded, he thought; as if she'd aged ten years during the night. Her face, which never had much colour, now resembled parchment and her eyes were underscored with black. She considered it suburban to appear downstairs before dressing, but here she was, wearing a dressing gown over a nightdress.

'I'd like some coffee if you could take the trouble to pour me a cup.'

'I'm afraid I didn't make more than the one cup.'

'Mug,' she contradicted. 'It didn't occur to you to think of me?'

It hadn't occurred to him that she would be down so early. Normally, when she had drunk more than was wise, she did not rise from her bed until well after he'd left the house. 'I'll make some more. Do you want anything to eat?'

She shook her head, winced.

He went through to the kitchen, emptied the grounds out of the coffee maker, washed that under the tap, filled the bowl with coffee and the base with water, screwed the two halves together and set the machine on the ceramic top of the two-oven cooker. A few moments later, it hissed. He'd had his coffee in a mug, but she liked standards to be observed so he put Meissen coffee pot, cup and saucer, silver teaspoon, milk jug, and sugar bowl, on a second tray, carried this through. He set everything in front of her. She did not thank him. He sat, finished buttering the toast, helped himself to marmalade, ate.

'Have you been reading the newspaper?' she asked.

He expected a comment on his poor social manners since she objected to his reading at breakfast, even after he'd assured her that aristocrats always read the newspapers at breakfast – he hadn't added that this was to prevent their having to listen to their wives.

'Is there any news?'

'The French are causing fresh trouble over Europe, but since they regard that as their God-given right, I don't suppose that's really news.'

'Why do you always—' She stopped abruptly. When she next spoke, she tried to moderate her abrasive tone. 'Is there any local news?'

'I haven't come across some. Would you expect there to be?'

'No.'

Then why ask? He finished the toast, drank the remaining coffee in his mug, checked the time. 'I must move. I'm presenting a proposed campaign for one of our most go-ahead clients and I want to make certain everything's a hundred per cent.' He stood. 'Sadly, it'll probably all be wasted effort. The chairman is almost certain to reject it on the grounds of dubious taste.' She made no comment. He wondered if it had ever occurred to her to offer him a little encouragement? He put mug, plates, cutlery, butter, jam, marmalade and toast rack on one tray, carried this through to the kitchen.

Enid had just arrived. He wished her a cheerful good morning; her reply suggested her morning was fog-laden. She'd worked for them for several years and he doubted he'd seen her cheerful more than a dozen times.

He went through the scullery and out to the courtyard and to his surprise saw that not only had Portia failed to garage her silver Mercedes E320, she had also not shut the road gates. Since security was one of her constant concerns, she must have been well and truly over the limit when she had driven back home. The Mercedes was partially blocking the right-hand garage in which was his Audi and so had to be moved. Car keys were normally kept in the kitchen for added safety, but in the circumstances she might well have left hers in the car. She had. He started the engine, activated the remote control and the left-hand garage door rose, at the same time swinging inwards. He backed to gain a better line into the garage and chanced to be looking along the bonnet as he straightened the wheel. He noticed the dent on the front offside wheel arch. At some stage of the evening she must have hit something, probably not too solid because as far as he could tell no paint had flaked off. Would she admit to the damage, or remain quiet, hoping he wouldn't notice? She liked to think of herself as a very safe, expert driver . . .

He hurried round to the Audi – time was becoming short and one could never be certain how much traffic there would be.

Detective Inspector Howes ran his hand over the top of his head, trying to smooth down the remaining hairs to conceal his baldness; he was not growing old either gracefully or resignedly. 'What do you make of things?'

Blundell shrugged his shoulders. 'Hard to say anything at the moment except it doesn't add up.'

Although they would both have heatedly denied the fact, they did have one thing in common; originally, each had been optimistically ambitious, but a lack of quick success and promotion had bred the resentful decision to find an easy route through the rest of his working life. Unsurprisingly, each saw the other as not quite up to the job.

'But the victim's dead, so we have to add it all up.' Howes picked up the typed report and began to read, then looked up. 'We're going to have to treat Maddock's evidence with great caution. He admits his eyesight is poor and measurements show he was some four hundred and sixty yards from the accident with the light fast going.'

'Even so, things point to the oncoming car travelling too quickly and well on its wrong side of the road. Sounds like a drunken driver.'

'Likely. It would explain how the woman came to be hit. I can't see anything to say whether the oncoming car's headlights were on. Rather important, wouldn't you think?'

Blundell hurried to divert criticism. 'Maddock's evidence was taken by a PC.'

'So I've read.'

Then have a shout at the inspector, not me, Blundell thought. 'I'll tell Roach to find out – he'll be questioning Maddock again later on.'

Howes put the report down on his desk. 'How is he coming along?'

'Inclined to think himself smarter than he really is.'

'That makes him a prospective candidate for top brass.'

Blundell managed a weak smile.

'Bearing Maddock's poor eyesight in mind, do we

accept there was a man in the car as well as the woman?'

'I don't see how Maddock could have imagined him.'

'Quite so. Was he the driver or a passenger?'

'Ten to one, the driver.'

'Why so?'

'Because men do the driving.'

'Rather a sexist conclusion.'

Blundell didn't know whether that was a serious remark.

'He examined the woman when she lay on the road after the accident, so must have seen she was very badly injured about the head. Why didn't he call for help? Why did he just clear off?'

'There's no saying.'

'What was he picking up at the rear of the car before he left?'

'Maddock couldn't suggest what.'

'All questions and no answers . . . We could have done without this one.' It was a remark Howes frequently made. 'We have to identify the woman very quickly. As the PC who drew up this report –' Howes looked down and read briefly – 'as PC Swift points out, it's odd there were no papers in the car, even more odd that there was no handbag.'

'With all the snatching that goes on, some women don't carry 'em these days.'

'But they'll have a purse – a woman's not going to drive anywhere without a penny.'

'In case of need?'

'Not very humorous,' said Howes. 'Of course, the handbag could have been taken by the man – in which case, it was either theft or a need to conceal identity. Have you checked the latest Missing Persons lists?'

'There's no one could be her on the latest county one.'

'Is that an admission you haven't yet consulted the national one?'

Blundell gloomily stared down at his shoes and wondered what it was going to cost to buy a new pair. The uniform branch were issued with boots, the CID had to buy their own shoes. So were inequalities fostered.

'Has Swansea come through with the name of the Astra's registered owner?'

'Not yet.'

'Hurry 'em up.'

Might as well try to move Everest into China.

'Have we identified Maddock's so-called squire?'

'Not yet.'

'That seems to have become your mantra. You don't feel it's important even though it could well give us the make of the hit-and-run car?'

'I've told Roach to check out who the squire is when he speaks to Maddock.'

'The PC who first questioned him should have had the initiative to obtain a definite identification.'

'You can't expect a uniform to be a genius.'

'You should know by now that I do not appreciate that sort of comment. It promotes a continuing ill-feeling between the two branches. We are all in the same team.'

Would the old fart now start talking about playing the game?

The chairman of Andrew & Sachs had missed the meeting because he was in bed with, as he had told his secretary, a very bad cold; he took great care of his health in order to preserve himself for the world. In his absence, the atmosphere of the get-together had been relaxed and the proposed campaign had, to Frayne's surprise, been considered solely on its merits; it had been approved for submission to the clients. In this day and age, one of the other directors had remarked, a boob was seldom a booboo.

He was seated at his desk, working on one of the

small changes suggested at the meeting, when Sandra entered. 'The local rag's in.' She put a newspaper down on his desk.

'Thanks . . . How did the birthday party go?'

'Like a dream.'

'It's now very hazy?'

She smiled.

He couldn't explain why, but her smile made him think she must be enthusiastic in bed. He watched her leave and noted how the movements of her buttocks – exaggerated for his benefit? – rippled the back of her dress. Portia would have named her tartish. At least tarts were sweet while vinegar was sour.

He looked through the Wednesday edition of the *Fretstone Gazette*, marking those advertisements and textual references which were of interest. The majority of advertising agencies aimed for the major markets; George Andrew, founder of Andrew & Sachs, had had the forethought to judge that there were good benefits to be gained from minor ones. Many a mickle makes a muckle. (The chairman, a pedant, would have very quickly pointed out the stupidity of that common saying.) Over the years, the firm had gained many clients who were attracted by the personal attention they were accorded even though they were, by many standards, tiny fish in a large ocean . . .

He noticed a Late News headline. 'Woman killed in hit-and-run.' He read the report. A woman, as yet unidentified, had been hit by a car which had not stopped; she had been pronounced dead on arrival at Fretstone General Hospital. The accident had happened just after ten the previous evening on the road between High Barnfield and Fretstone and the police were asking anyone who had been on that road at around that time to get in touch with them. Mr Peter Maddock who had witnessed the accident said the oncoming car had been driving at very great speed and all over the road and it had been truly horrible to see the woman thrown around like a rag doll. He added that a man who had also been in the car had left the scene. When asked about this man, the police spokesman stated that he could give no information concerning him. If anyone knew of a missing woman, aged about 35, wavy, dyed blonde hair, blue eyes, about 5′ 8″ in height and 8 to 9 stone in weight, dressed in a red and green print dress, would they please get in touch with the police.

He turned the page. Fretstone had, by letters patent, recently been given the status of city and the newly appointed mayor occupied a four-column-wide photograph; gold chain of office was in evidence as he stepped out of a newly acquired, pre-owned Rolls-Royce, a smirk of satisfaction shaping his mouth. Probably wondering how heavy a crown would feel, Frayne thought.

He skimmed through the remaining pages, folded the newspaper. It occurred to him that Winifred lived on the outskirts of High Barnfield and so if Portia had visited her the previous evening she would have been on the road at about the time in question. Since the police probably wanted the evidence of anyone who might have seen the car which ran the woman down, she should let them know . . . He was reminded of one of Portia's more objectionable sayings, Bungalows are lived in by bungalow people. Winifred might now live in a bungalow, but she had started life in a manor house.

Seven

B lundell distrusted Roach, who had recently been appointed detective constable having completed his stint as aide. He was always wary of those with very active imaginations since it was they who caused the problems of the world; being content to bow his head to authority, he couldn't understand those who weren't; having settled for doing whatever common sense and self-interest suggested, he was embarrassed, sometimes even humiliated, by someone who possessed that quality of stubborn belief which could drive him on, regardless of where his own interests lay. 'When you have a name, find out what make of car he owns.'

'Will do,' Roach said.

'And don't take all day.'

'No dallying with the maidens on the village green?'

'You won't get the chance if they've any taste.'

Roach left and went along the corridor to the CID general room. He entered, passed the wall-mounted board covered with a jumble of notices and photographs calling for identification of ringed subjects, stepped around a pile of books on the floor, threaded his way between several empty desks to reach his own. He collected up the papers on which he'd been working and returned them to a file. He accepted that some paperwork was essential, but was convinced, as were most, that it had grown like a tumour until it was interfering with, rather than merely recording, police work. By the time a man appeared in court, there could have been thirty-two forms which had had to be carefully filled in.

He left, returned along the passage past the detective sergeant's and the detective inspector's rooms, to the landing. The left-hand lift was restricted for the use of those with the rank of DI and above. It amused him that while externally maintaining democracy, internally the force delighted in maintaining the trappings of hierarchy. On the ground floor, he walked briskly out to the car park. The CID cars were all out, so he crossed to his Fiesta and settled behind the wheel, then wrote in his notebook that at 1535 hours, with the car's milometer recording 65,987 miles, he left Divisional HQ to make enquiries. Later, he would make a claim for motoring expenses which would be queried – it always was; Accounts seemed to think every policeman was on the make. A fact which initially he had resented. But it hadn't taken long to learn that even among honest men, honesty possessed elasticity. There were those who always added a few miles to their claims and found good reasons to justify them . . . He replaced notebook and pen, started the engine, drove to the exit and when the road was clear, turned on to it.

He chose a slightly roundabout route because this took him through West Neatford, a small town which time seemed to have forgotten – the high street was lined with independent shops which still offered service and quality, and it was several months since a public telephone had been vandalized. A fortnight before, Hazel and he had driven through there and as they'd passed one of the large Carolean/Georgian houses – architecture was not his forte – she'd said she'd sell her soul to live in such a home. It was not her soul which most interested him. If he won the lottery, he'd buy one of those houses and marry her, thereby cutting short her friendship with the long-haired, pasty-faced git whose only claim to value was a rich father . . . As he came abreast of the last house on the outskirts, he accepted it had been a mistake to drive through the small town in order to revive and relive memories – all it had done was to remind him that he didn't drive a Jaguar and couldn't afford to take Hazel to La Tour d'Artoise where a man could be presented with a bill for a hundred and fifty pounds after a meal for two.

Ten minutes later, a sign warned of a sharp bend ahead. He slowed the car and drove around the corner with even greater care than was needed. Ahead of him there now lay a straight stretch of road. Less than twenty-four hours before, someone had come out of the corner far too quickly, had swerved this way and that, had slammed into a woman who'd been on the road on the offside of a car which had suffered a puncture. She had died instantly, or soon afterwards. It disturbed him that death could arrive so unexpectedly and pointlessly; that the driver of the other car had almost certainly been drunk; that having struck the woman, he had been so callous as not to stop and give what assistance he could. Perhaps in time, Roach assured himself, he would have suffered sufficient experience not to be disturbed by the irrationality of fate or the stupidity of humans . . .

He braked to a halt in front of the small cottage. The flower beds were full of colour and the small lawn had the appearance of green velvet. If he could somehow find the money, and mortgage, to buy a place like this (forget that lottery win), would Hazel – a keen gardener so she could do all the gardening – forgo her dreams of Carolean/Georgian magnificence?

As he opened the front gate, Maddock came round the side of the house, brushing his hands together to free them of dirt. Roach introduced himself.

'It's more questions, then?'

'I'm afraid so.'

'Best come inside.'

They entered the small hall and Maddock called out;

his wife came through from the kitchen. 'Another copper, Ma.'

'Then go through to the front room. And how about some tea?'

'I'm afraid I don't like tea,' Roach said. 'I only drink coffee.'

'That's all right, there's just a little of the instant left in the jar from when our Greg was here with the family four months back.'

'More like two months,' Maddock said, as he settled heavily in one of the armchairs.

'Never knows how long ago anything was,' she said to Roach. 'And always arguing. Tell him it's dark and he says it ain't, but won't look to find out . . . I'll go and make the coffee.'

A small amount of instant coffee left in the bottom of a jar for four months was not going to taste as advertisements promised, Roach thought; it was a great pity that politeness didn't allow him to point that out.

Maddock said: 'You'll be wanting to know what happened. I'll tell you. I was doing some gardening even though it was late and getting dark because her was on about the weeds in the flower beds. I don't mind weeding the kitchen garden 'cause I eats vegetables, but I don't eat roses and lupins—'

Roach interrupted and asked what the other had seen of the accident. Maddock's description was so voluble it was obvious it had been polished and enlarged by repetition.

Mrs Maddock brought in coffee for him, tea for her husband and herself, biscuits for all. The coffee proved to be tasteless, which in the circumstances was a relief. As Maddock noisily drank tea, Roach said: 'When you spoke to the PC last night, you didn't mention whether the car that hit the victim had its headlights on.'

'I didn't?' Maddock held the cup in front of his mouth. 'Must have done, mustn't it, since it was getting dark.'

'But you can't be certain?'

'Yes, I can. They was on.' He finished his tea with a last burst of slurping sound.

Maybe yes, maybe no, Roach thought. 'And the single letter of the number plate was definitely X?'

'Like I told the copper last night.'

'You described the car as looking like the squire's. How similar would you judge it to have been?'

'The spitting image. The same colour, the same everything.'

'You know, it can be rather difficult to judge colour when the light's going.'

'It ain't for me.'

'Do you wear glasses?'

'Just to read. And I don't need glasses to tell what colour a car is, and that's fact, that is.'

She said: 'Steady on, Dad. The policeman has to make certain.'

'Not when I say.'

She turned to Roach. 'He can be terrible obstinate.'

'It's you what never listen,' Maddock protested.

She helped herself to another biscuit.

'Who is the person you call the squire?' Roach asked.

'The squire, of course.'

Ask a simple question . . . 'But what is his real name?'

'Mr Chadwick. Only you'll understand, he ain't a proper squire. I can remember when it were Mr Tallboy in the big house. A real gentleman . . .'

Roach listened to the description of a man who seemingly had reached the status of blessed and would soon have been in sight of a sainthood. Yet in the books he'd read, the squires had chased the village maidens and horsewhipped those who tried to prevent their enjoying what they considered to be their rights. 'Where does Mr Chadwick live?'

'In the big house, of course.' Maddock clearly scorned dull intelligence.

'Where is the big house?' Roach asked, with commend-able patience.

She answered him. 'A mile up the road, there's a turning to the left and another mile further on there's some gates and the house lies back of 'em. And you need to watch out for the dogs. Nell, what works there, says as they're dangerous.'

'That's only 'cause she don't know how to handle dogs,' Maddock said aggressively.

'And you're saying you do?'

'That's right.'

'Then suppose you go up there when they're let out and teach 'em how to behave?'

'If they bite, I'll sue.'

'If you know all about handling 'em, they won't bite, will they?'

Maddock muttered something that was unintelligible.

Roach drank half the coffee remaining in his cup and decided he could politely leave what now remained. He thanked them for their help, left.

Beyond the Maddock's cottage was an easy bend, a much shorter straight, another bend and a turning to the left. Half a mile further on – not the mile quoted – an eight-foot brick wall began and he reached a gateway with intricate wrought-iron gates.

The drive passed between centuries-old oak trees to end in a gravel-surfaced turning area, in the centre of which was a raised flower bed. The house was large, old and, to judge from the irregular form of the front, had been subjected to several alterations and additions over the centuries. What would Hazel do if he brought her here and told her it was his? Throw herself into his arms and for once forget how to say, 'You musn't . . .'?

He crossed to the large portico. The front door was seven feet tall, heavily panelled and studded – it might have been designed to withstand a siege. On the door was a wrought-iron knocker in the form of a staghound and, to the side, an electric bell. Being essentially a traditionist, he used the knocker. It made a deep, reverberating sound that made him think of the hammer of doom. Would the door be opened by an ancient, skeletal man with eye teeth very much longer than normal? Twenty seconds later, he was faced by an attractive woman in her late twenties who wore a frock with sufficient décolletage to provide interest.

'Sorry to bother you, but I'm making enquiries. Detective Constable Roach, county CID. Is Mr Chadwick at home?'

'No, he isn't. He's in London.'

'Then maybe you can help me. You are . . . ?'

'Linda O'Duffey. I'm his personal assistant.'

If he were wealthy enough to own a house like this, he'd have an assistant who was very personal. 'Perhaps you can tell me what make of car Mr Chadwick owns?'

'Why?'

'Not because there's any suggestion of trouble as far as he's concerned.' He smiled to suggest no idea could be more ridiculous. 'But it's to provide a comparison.'

After a moment, she said. 'You'd better come on in.'

He stepped into a hall of baronial proportions on the walls of which hung mounted heads of various animals. One of the 'real' squires must have shot his way from Cairo to Cape Town. He followed her into a panelled room that looked out onto the park. A man could stand at the window and truly say, 'I am monarch of all I survey . . .' He could remember neither the next line nor the name of the author.

'You say you wish to know what make of car Mr Chadwick owns?'

'That's right.'

'I'm not certain I should give you the information.'

'He hasn't been caught doing thirty-one in a thirty area.'

'As chairman of the society dedicated to lower speed limits in towns in order to reduce accidents, he's hardly likely to have been speeding.'

He wondered if her husband found her a little on the sharp side. 'It's this way, there's been a fatal accident in which a car that didn't stop was involved and a witness has described the car as exactly similar to Mr Chadwick's, so if we know what he owns, we'll know the make and, hopefully, the model of the car we're looking for.'

'In that case, there can't be any objection to my telling you. He and his wife own three cars. A Bentley, a Mercedes, and a Range Rover.'

Conspicuous consumption. 'Is one of them silver coloured?'

'The Mercedes.'

'Can you say what model it is?'

'Not off-hand. But if I check through some papers, I almost certainly will be able to.'

'Would you be kind enough to do that?'

She left.

He turned and looked out at the park. All that was lacking to complete the traditional scene was a herd of deer. Perhaps it was they, and not African exotica, which stared glassy-eyed down from the walls of the hall.

She returned. 'It's called an E three-twenty. Does that help?'

'It certainly does . . . It's a lovely view, isn't it? Was there once a herd of deer?'

'I couldn't say.'

It was a long time since he had so evidently failed to charm. Was youth already deserting him?

Eight

B lundell checked the time and was gratified to note it
would soon be OK to head for home. DIs hot on the
promotion trail would try to work everyone all hours God
made even if financial limits had been reached and there
could be no overtime, but Howes, accepting there would
be no further promotion, was more relaxed.

The phone rang.

'Vehicles here. The number you gave us of an Astra
identifies it as stolen three days ago.'

'That was not on the cards!'

'Don't they say, "Always expect the unexpected"?'

'I expect some silly sod does. Stolen from where?'

'Minestone.'

'Where's that?'

'Sussex.'

'What were the circumstances?'

'It was in the drive of the house when the owner went
to bed, missing when he got up. No one heard a thing even
though the car's supposed to have an alarm that can't be
bypassed.'

'Tell that to any chummy and hear him choke from
laughing.'

'The odd thing is, we're seeing a pattern change. Yesterday, it was prestige cars disappeared, today, it's run of the
mill ones. Like as not, most of 'em are for cannibalization.'

Blundell brought the conversation to an end with brief

thanks. He replaced the receiver. It seemed obvious why, after the woman had been hit, the man had picked up something and fled, careless as to whether she was still alive and quick medical attention might save her life. Was there a known house-team which consisted of a man and a woman? Off-hand, he couldn't think of one.

If Howes was still around, he'd want to know exactly where Minestone was – he always hoped to give the impression of efficiency by concentrating on detail, whether or not that was relevant. Blundell swivelled his chair round and brought out from the glass-fronted bookcase a road map with a good gazetteer of the British Isles. This told him that Minestone was a few miles south of Gatwick airport. He lacked the constructive imagination to wonder if there could be any significance in that fact.

He walked through to the DI's office and was chuffed to find it empty. He wrote a brief note recording the phone call, carefully added the location of the town to show he was on the ball, positioned the sheet of paper on the desk so that it lay square to the four sides. As with many small-minded men, Howes demanded geometric tidiness.

Frayne opened the road gates by remote control, drove into the courtyard, opened the right-hand garage by remote, drove into the garage. Before long, life would no doubt be lived by remote control.

Briefcase in one hand, he crossed the courtyard and entered the house through the scullery. The kitchen was empty and Portia was not in the blue room, seated in front of the television and watching one of the soaps to which she seemed addicted. He went upstairs and along the corridor to her room, opened the door. She was in bed.

'Who is it?' she called out, her voice fuzzy.

'Who would you like it to be? Or is that an indelicate question?'

Her bed was a half-tester, bought by her in a sale at

a country mansion in Shropshire because – so he was convinced – it had been asserted that the Prince Regent had once slept in it on a visit.

She looked bleary-eyed as she sat up. 'Do you always have to be facetious?' she demanded angrily. 'And why couldn't you knock?'

'I didn't realize that was necessary.'

'You don't think I'm entitled to some privacy?'

'To all you want. I only came up because I wondered if you were all right.'

'Why shouldn't I be?'

'You weren't downstairs.'

'You can't appreciate that with all I have to do running a large house, I sometimes get tired?'

There would have been less to do in that converted oast house. But no doubt her hangovers would have been just as exhausting. 'I'm glad there's nothing seriously wrong with you. Can I get you anything?'

'No.'

'If you could manage a light meal it would help settle things.'

'Are you trying to suggest I drank too much?'

'Such a thought couldn't cross my mind.'

'Anything that discredits me crosses your mind.'

'That's nonsense. Portia . . .'

'I'm going to get up. Would you leave so I can get dressed?'

'You can't do that whilst I'm in the room?'

'I've no wish to have you leering at me.'

It was a long time since he had looked at her with any real desire – for there to be desire, there had to be some hope of its being granted.

Downstairs, he poured himself a strong gin and tonic in the butler's pantry, then went through to the blue room, sat, and switched on the television. He changed channels three times, found nothing worth watching, and switched off.

Portia entered, dressed in an expensive summer frock that would have looked elegant on someone younger, slimmer, and happier. She sat.

'Can I get you something to drink?'

She looked at him with sharp, suspicious dislike. 'No.'

'You remember I told you that today I was going to present proposals for a fairly important campaign?'

She didn't bother to answer.

'*Mirabile dictu*, the chairman was ill in bed – unfortunately not suffering from anything serious – and the board accepted my proposals subject to a few minor alterations.' He waited for a comment, any comment, but there was none. 'Since it's one of our major clients and I've been working on my own, modesty compels me to admit that that's something of a feather in my cap.'

'Then maybe they'll give you a proper salary so you can start paying your share of the house expenses.'

She seldom lost the chance to sneer at the reasonable, if not generous, salary he was paid or that it was she who met all the daily costs of running Bell's House. When riding in a Rolls, it was all too easy to be contemptuous of the man in the Mini. He stood and left the room to refill his glass. When he returned, he said, 'That reminds me. Were you at Winifred's last night?'

'Why d'you ask?' Her tone was sharp.

'Because if you were . . .'

'It's none of your business. When I want to see Winifred, I will.'

'Who am I to object?'

'Then stop insinuating.'

'I was insinuating nothing. And before you suggest it, my reason for asking wasn't prurient curiosity.'

'Why do you say prurient?'

Because there were times when his tongue lacked a sense of discretion. 'Only because all curiosity, by its very nature, is prurient . . . Why I wondered if you'd been at her place was that if you had, you'd have driven along Potters Road on your way home.'

'I didn't visit her and I wasn't on that road last night. But what if I had been?'

'There was a fatal accident and the police are asking anyone who was on the road around ten and a quarter past to get in touch with them. It's fairly obvious the driver was drunk, so I suppose they want any report on how the car was being driven before the accident.'

'It's no concern of mine since I wasn't anywhere near there. It's so typical of you to think I was.'

'All I thought . . .'

'I'm going back to bed.'

'I'm sure you'd feel better if you'd have something to eat. Suppose I open a tin of chicken soup and add some of those garlic croutons . . .'

She stood and hurried out.

Her attitude had been as aggressive as in the morning . . . She claimed not to have visited Winifred the previous evening, but if true, where had she been to become so inebriated? Normally, when she was in someone else's home – that was, someone she considered to be of consequence – she made a point of not accepting a second drink because a lady (or someone who wished to be considered a lady) was always seen to be content with one. And then he remembered a second social convention had been cast aside when she had come downstairs in a dressing-gown and nightdress. Equally strange, she'd asked him what local news there was in the newspaper. What local news could she have expected to appear in *The Times*?

His thoughts coalesced. When he'd said that had she been at Winifred's, her return to Bell's House would have placed her on Potters Road at around the time of the crash and so she should get in touch with the police, she had angrily denied having visited Winifred's and he had seemed to discern something beyond anger in her tone – had that something been fear? The report said the victim had been hit by the oncoming car's off-side. The Mercedes had a dent on the off-side wheel arch, but no paint had been flaked off, suggesting an object that yielded rather than one that was totally solid . . . He silently swore. Was his ability to distort or invent circumstances to point suspicion an indication that deep within his mind there was so strong a dislike that he would welcome proof of her involvement in the fatal hit-and-run?

Nine

Howes said, as always taking care over his pronunciation, 'So now we can surmise why the man picked up something and then cleared off, leaving her dead or dying. The two of them had been on a job.'

'It certainly looks that way.' Blundell fidgeted with the ring on his marriage finger. His father would have poured scorn on his wearing it, his son thought it uncool because it was so plain, he would have preferred to be free of it, but his wife had asked him to wear it. She was someone who was forever taking steps to prevent the worst occurring. In truth, he had never cheated and never would, though many a tom had offered herself in exchange for a blind eye.

'Have you checked the night's break-ins?'

'Yes, sir. That is, the county ones – the list is there, on your desk. I've asked for reports from surrounding forces, but there's none come through yet.'

'Too damned lazy to move.'

Had there ever been a force which awarded anything but low priority to a request for information that would entail work which came from another force?

'Since the car was heading westwards, it's reasonable to assume the break-in was to the east.'

'Which makes four local jobs possible.'

'Is there anything to pick out one of them?'

'Not so far.'

Howes fingered the sheet of paper on which the list had been printed out; he rolled one corner between finger and thumb. Will there be any immediate benefit to identifying the likely target? he asked himself. Then he said aloud: 'I don't recall any man and woman team. Do you?'

'I've never come across a mixed one.'

'There's obviously still some sex discrimination in the county.'

Blundell managed to raise a weak smile.

'The odds must be, they have form. Have you arranged for her dabs to be taken?'

'Not yet.'

'Why not?'

'The information came in too late yesterday evening to organize things with the coroner's office. And when I was detailing Lipman this morning, news came through that one of the town councillors has been mugged on his way to work and his gold Rolex nicked, so I had to send Lipman there. Being short-staffed with one man sick, another—'

'Which town councillor?'

'Tobin.'

'The man who gives us stick because he reckons we're forever breaching human rights? I'll guarantee that if we don't retrieve his watch quickly, he'll be shouting for every known mugger to be hauled in and put on the rack. There's nothing changes a liberal so completely as suffering what he's been excusing.'

'We're not going to make any ground on this one. Tobin's all at sea when it comes to the facts and his description of the mugger sounds like he was having a nightmare.'

Howes rested his elbows on the desk. 'To expect defeat is to be defeated.'

And save a lot of mental frustration.

In his office, Frayne doodled on a sheet of rough paper. Could the continuing consideration of an absurdity betray the dark corners of a mind? Where would Portia have been drinking so heavily as she had been other than at Winifred's; was it pure coincidence that if she had driven back along Potters Road within a very short time of the accident, she would have arrived home at the time she did: why had she been so apparently emotionally disturbed the following morning that she had come downstairs in night clothes and asked whether there was any local news in the paper; what had caused the dent on the Mercedes . . . ?

Sandra came into the room. 'Is the typing ready, Dick?'

He dropped the pencil onto the desk. 'Not yet.'

'I thought it was rather urgent?'

'It is. But I've been day-dreaming about living on a tropical island and watching coconuts fall.'

'You might take me with you.'

'Wouldn't Tom object?'

'Not if I promise to behave.'

'Then what's the point in your coming?'

She smiled. 'I'll look in again in half an hour.' She left, closed the door behind herself.

He pushed aside the paper on which he'd been doodling, opened a folder and riffled through the papers inside, found the one he wanted. Questions demanding answers. How much of the proposed budget for the campaign now being sized would be eaten up by three, six, or nine consecutive thirty/sixty-second slots during the advertising break in the half-hour of local TV news? Did the projected increase in sales following TV exposure warrant the expenditure, having regard to the fact that newspaper advertising would be greatly reduced? Would TV exposure have little viable impact if the smallest number of slots was chosen in order that newspaper advertising should be not too greatly cut back . . . ?

Did he give a damn when his mind was circling infinitely more important questions?

He picked up the receiver to the outside line, replaced it. If Portia learned why he'd phoned Winifred, she'd be furious. So he had to find a way of gaining an answer without raising sufficient curiosity for Winifred later to ask Portia what was up. He lifted the receiver again and went to dial, found his mind had gone so blank he could not remember the number. Was his subconscious warning him not to phone because the consequences could be catastrophic? . . . Pull yourself together, he angrily told himself. He dialled.

'Yes?'

Her manner was always abrupt, often to the point of rudeness. 'It's Dick.'

'Dick who?'

'How about Turpin?'

'Only one man I know has that kind of warped humour. What do you want?'

'Portia's in a state because she's lost her purse. I've tried to help, but been blasted for my pains so I daren't suggest it to her, but can ask you. Did she leave it at your place Tuesday night?'

'She's only just discovered it's missing?'

'She has a purse for each handbag and swaps handbags around . . . I'll be eternally in your debt if you tell me, but not her.'

'Eternal debts never get paid. If she had one practical purse and handbag instead of all those smart and bloody useless ones, she wouldn't lose things.'

Whatever the nature of their friendship – a question he avoided – there were times when there was clearly a degree of resentment on Winifred's part, almost certainly caused by their different financial situations. 'Have you found her purse?'

'I've already answered you.'

'I don't think so.'

'Portia says you spend your life arguing.'

'Only because I'm always in the right.'

'Cocky bastard!' she said approvingly.

'Born in strict wedlock . . . Have you found it?'

'If I had, I'd have told her so.'

With much comment on carelessness, no doubt. 'Fair enough. So now to more important things. How are you?'

'How d'you expect me to be?'

'The kind of question no sensible man ever answers.'

'You can be a smooth bastard!'

'I'm overwhelmed by the compliments.'

She laughed, sounding rather like a seal barking.

'I must hie me back to work. Sorry to have troubled you.'

'Any time.'

He said goodbye, rang off. She hadn't confirmed that Portia had been with her on Tuesday evening, but nor had she denied it. Her nature was always to correct others. The phone call made to rid his mind of an absurd suspicion had merely made it seem that much less absurd.

Lipman watched the mortuary assistant slide out one of the fifteen refrigerated compartments and transfer the sheeted body onto the trolley which had been adjusted to the necessary height. He knew that tonight he would drink far too much to try to overcome the scene now before him. He was scared of death; not of just his own, but of its very concept. For him, death was the black hole which made a mockery of all life every time it sucked a soul into nothingness.

The assistant wheeled the trolley towards the autopsy room and as he edged it through the doorway, an arm flopped out from under the white sheet and hung down. 'She's saying hullo.'

Lipman would have liked to hit him.

The assistant manoeuvred the trolley alongside the nearer stainless-steel table on which bodies were placed for an autopsy to be carried out. He switched on the pod of overhead lights.

The floor and walls were washed down and disinfected after each autopsy, but the scent of death could not be removed; at least, not for Lipman.

'So is forensic coming or do we spend the rest of the day waiting?'

'He said he'd be here at half past.'

'It's twenty to. Still, she ain't in no rush.'

Perhaps, Lipman thought, a man could only reconcile himself to facing death every working day if he made a joke of it. He wished he could learn the secret of how to do that.

The right-hand door opened and a tall, lanky man hurried in. 'Traffic's thicker than bees round a honey pot,' he muttered as he put a case down on the floor. 'In five years' time, it'll be gridlock from one end of the town to the other . . . Reg Lipman, isn't it?'

'That's right.'

'Never forget a face or a name . . . Mine's Moon.' He leaned down, snapped open the two locks of the case, lifted the lid, brought out a transparent bag in which was a white surgical gown.

'No need for that, surely?' said the mortuary assistant.

'Habit.' For him, there were no short cuts.

The mortuary assistant pulled the sheet down to reveal the naked body from the waist upwards. 'A nice pair gone to waste.'

Lipman silently cursed the other.

Moon checked the two hands of the corpse, making certain each was sufficiently unclenched. He used a small rubber roller to ink the thumb of the right hand, put a shaped piece of paper on a wooden 'spoon', slowly and evenly rolled this across the thumb. He removed the paper, carefully placed it in a plastic box that inside was shaped with ten indentations the size and shape of the piece of paper and a lid which, when lowered, would hold all the papers in place without touching the prints. He repeated this nine times more. He replaced roller, wooden 'spoon', and ink pad in the suitcase, took off his gown and stuffed it into a plastic bag. He stuck a label on the box in which were the prints and wrote on this the time, date, place, 'Unknown Victim', and signed it. He motioned to Lipman to add his signature.

Several minutes later, Lipman left the building. He came to a stop in front of the lilac tree – the small garden between the building and the pavement was supposed to counter any unwelcome emotions amongst the public – and breathed deeply, the sunshine catching his face at an angle and highlighting the scar on his chin, caused by a knife which had been meant to kill him.

On Monday morning, Howes's mind was far away when Roach entered his office. Regretfully, he ceased planning his retirement.

'The list from Swansea of county-registered silver Mercedes E three-twenties has just come through, sir,' Roach reported.

'Let's have it.' Howes quickly read through the several names and addresses. He put it down on his desk, sat back in the chair. 'Of course, there's no certainty the car is locally owned, but it seems likely since Potters Road is very much in the country and unlikely to be used by someone who doesn't know the area well.' He began to tap his fingers on the desk. 'We're short staffed and following up enquiries will take manpower we haven't got.'

They'd have greater manpower available if both the DI and the DS got off their backsides more often, Roach thought.

'What's the name of the man who saw this car?'

'Maddock.'

'I wonder how reliable his identification of the car really is? Not easy these days to tell one make from another, very difficult when it's a case of distinguishing two models of the same make.'

'Maddock is a real countryman; maybe not as smart as many, but he'll have very good powers of discriminatory observation. He'll be able to identify each sheep in a flock when to you and me they all look the same. If he says the car he saw exactly matches the one Mr Chadwick owns, I'd guess it almost certainly was a Merc three-twenty that killed the woman.'

Howes stopped tapping his fingers. 'Time spent on this case means less spent on others because the government can't understand that good policing costs. But what politician does understand money can only be spent once? . . . Tell Sergeant Blundell to have all the cars on this list checked.' He picked up the sheet of paper and held it out.

Roach left. Blundell was not in his office, so he continued on to the general room. Only Oakes was present. 'D'you know where the skipper is, Ken?' he asked.

Oakes, who had somehow just wiped from the PC in front of him his last fifteen minutes of typing, said in purple prose that he didn't.

'Are you doing anything?'

'Do I look as if I'm sodding well sitting with the girlfriend, enjoying life?'

'No, which means she probably is . . . The DI says the owners on this list of silver Mercs are to be questioned to find out if maybe it was one of them ran the woman down in Potters Road. The skipper will have to decide who does the asking.'

Anything was preferable to a malfunctioning computer. 'We'll show we're stuffed full of initiative.' Oakes stood.

That Lynch lived luxuriously was not readily apparent. Seen from the road, the house was not particularly large, certainly not grand, and it dated from the thirties, when style had not played much of a part in bourgeois values.

Inside, however, there was expensive beauty. He had a love of antique furniture and the eye to distinguish the good from the not so good, the not so good from the fake; he knew enough about paintings to have assembled a small collection that a minor museum would have been happy to accept; his collection of gold and silver snuff boxes included one that had been made by Fabergé for Czar Nicholas II; valuable silk prayer carpets hung on the walls . . .

'So add it up,' he said sharply.

Benson, small, wiry, with eyes which seldom remained fixed on anything and certainly never on anyone, answered. 'She'll stay in the morgue until the driver of the car is identified and tried.'

'Has she been opened up?'

'My informant says not, which sounds right. Her head was busted on the parked car so cause of death was obvious. In such cases, there's no legal need for a full autopsy.'

'So when does the driver come up in court?'

'There's no saying.'

'I pay you to say.'

Benson moved uneasily in the luxuriously upholstered, leather-covered chair. To look at Lynch was to see over-weight hedonism; to know him was to recognize monumental self-interest, great covetousness, and a vicious indifference to the consequences of anything he did or ordered to be done.

The door opened and Ferdinand, in his middle twenties, handsome despite, or because of, features touched with femininity, dressed with casual chic, entered, then came to a sharp halt. 'Didn't know you were busy.'

'You do now,' Lynch snapped.

'Is that a little hint for me to leave?'

'Three words to tell you to get the hell out of here.'

Ferdinand left, a petulant expression on his face.

'Well?' demanded Lynch.

'How's that, Esme?' Benson asked.

'Why don't you know when there'll be the trial?'

'I can't say how the police investigation is going . . .'

'Why not?'

'I've no direct lead.'

'Then find one.'

'It's not that easy. I'll do all I can, of course. And you have to understand that maybe the police won't be able to trace the car and identify the driver quickly so she could be kept on ice for a long time.'

'She's got to come out quick. I borrowed heavy, it's costing, and the people who covered me get very uneasy if they don't get repaid on time.'

Big fleas had bigger fleas upon their backs to bite them, Benson thought, not without considerable gratification.

Ten

S aturday brought warm sunshine and the lightest of
breezes. Frayne crossed the lawn to where Mercer
was weeding one of the herbaceous borders and began
to chat to him – Mercer was not a very intelligent man,
but he possessed such gardening skills that he could plant
a twig today and all but have a tree growing tomorrow.
They heard a car drive into the courtyard. Frayne said:
'I'm not expecting anyone so I'd better find out who that
is. Maybe someone collecting for the church fête . . . Is
your wife making cherry jam for that?'

'Aye.' Mercer was not a ready speaker.

'I must make certain we buy some. Beats the shop stuff
hollow.' He turned and made his way to the parked car
and the well-built man with a humorously lined face who
had stepped out of it. 'Good morning.'

'Mr Frayne?'

'That's right.'

'Detective Constable Roach, local CID.'

'Not collecting for the church fête!'

'I'm sorry?'

Frayne smiled. 'I didn't recognize the car and, as one
often does, was trying to guess who you were. Come along
in and tell me what's brought you here.'

He led the way along a passage which bypassed the
kitchen and gave direct access to the hall. In the blue
room, he said: 'Have a seat. And can I offer you something
to drink?'

'No, thanks.'

'Then how can I help you?'

'I'm making enquiries following a road accident nearly a fortnight ago.'

Frayne wondered how he could have been so lulled by summer's murmur as to fail to realize this was the likely cause for the visit. He said, doing his best to keep his voice level: 'Was it a bad accident?'

'Very nasty. A woman was killed by a hit-and-run driver. I'm here because we have reason to think the car in question was a silver Mercedes and so we're contacting every local owner of such a car to see if we can eliminate it. Records show that your wife took delivery of a silver Mercedes E three-twenty a little while back.'

'It sounds as if you're trying to identify rather than eliminate.'

'By doing the latter often enough, we hope to succeed with the former.'

'And it's less intimidating to talk about eliminating?'

Roach smiled.

'You'd like to eliminate my wife's car?'

'That's right.'

'Unfortunately, she's out in it and I don't expect her back until this evening.'

'Then I'll come back another time. When will be convenient?'

'How about tomorrow morning, around about ten thirty? That's if you're on duty on Sundays?'

'Unfortunately, our working weeks have eight days.'

'Very tiring! . . . Then tomorrow morning it is. I'm afraid it'll be a wasted journey.'

'We often prefer it that way, Mr Frayne.'

'But obviously, not always! . . . Tell me, as a matter of interest, how will you hope to identify the car in question?'

'There'll be signs of contact.'

'What exactly does that mean?'

'The metal somewhere will almost certainly be deformed, there could be a pattern on the paintwork corresponding to the clothing the woman was wearing, paint may be missing . . . There's always something.'

'Always?'

'That's what the scientists claim. So if we can't find anything, it's assumed we're half blind.' He stood. 'Thanks for your help.'

'Only too glad to do anything I can.'

Frayne went through to the courtyard with Roach, said goodbye, watched the car leave. He hurried back into the house and went through to the hall, dialled the number of Portia's mobile. After several rings, her recorded voice, filled with refined vowels, asked the caller to leave a message after the signal. He replaced the receiver. Would she ever learn to switch on the mobile when she went out?

Roach entered Blundell's room.

'Where the hell have you been?' Blundell demanded.

'Checking up on the last of the Mercs.'

'Taken your time . . . Any joy?'

'No, because—'

'That's one job out of the way, then.'

'Hang on, Sarge. There was no joy because it's the wife's car and she was out in it. I've fixed up to go back tomorrow morning since I'm duty officer.'

'It didn't occur to you to check with me – having to get twenty men's work done by six – before deciding how you'll spend the morning?'

'The DI said he wanted the job finished as soon as possible, so I thought . . .'

'I'd have a bloody sight easier job if there were DCs who didn't think.'

'Then you want me to ring Mr Frayne and fix another day?'

'He won't want to be mucked around by the likes of you.'

'So I go there tomorrow?'

'And make it as quick as possible.'

Roach remained standing in front of the desk.

'Nothing to do?'

'There was something a bit odd about Mr Frayne.'

'Show me someone who's not bloody odd.'

'He's obviously wealthy – big house, big garden, probably a gardener – but he was pleasant even when I told him I wanted to check whether it was his wife's car was the hit-and-run vehicle.'

'You usually annoy the people you question?'

'Sarge, you know life – the wealthier or more important a person, the more indignant he becomes if it seems he could be suspected of anything. In no time flat, he's threatening libel.'

'Slander.'

'Another thing. He was interested in how we'll identify the car.'

'Those telly programmes make every half-wit think he's a dead ringer for detective superintendent.'

'He was relaxed at the beginning, then I explained why I was there and he was on edge.'

'How d'you know?'

'One can tell.'

'You think you can, which is a sight different.'

'Level up. One gets a feeling. I'll bet my reputation that the moment I mentioned the hit-and-run, he was sweating blood inside.'

'Your stake would make a gambler laugh.'

The report was brought to Howes as he was about to leave to go home and enjoy the weekend. The fingerprints of the deceased woman, identity previously unknown, named her Carol Fowler. Aged thirty-six, the mother of one daughter aged six. Arrested and fined three times for importuning, awarded a six-months suspended sentence for an assault on another prostitute. Last known address, 36 Lowcoat Avenue, Dukeston.

A tom. Who had joined with an unknown male to burgle country houses. Enquiries would have to be made regarding the welfare of the daughter and to find out if she had other relatives who would need to be consulted over the funeral arrangements when permission for burial was granted, but since Dukeston was in another county, that would be someone else's task.

He took the fax through to Blundell's room, wrote on one edge of it, 'Contact local force to identify other relatives, etc.', put it down exactly in the centre of the desk and then squared up a couple of files which had been lazily left anyhow.

Frayne was drinking his second Cinzano and soda of the evening when he heard the Mercedes drive into the court-yard. He hurried through the hall, kitchen, and scullery, reached Portia as she stood outside the garage and pressed the control to lower the door. 'I tried to get you on the mobile. I rang Vera and Harriet to find out if you were with either of them.'

'Really? I decided to go up to London and have lunch with Ingrid. What a frumpy woman she's become since she had that beastly child which snivels all the time . . . You can bring the bags in.' She indicated with a nod of her head the two carrier bags that bore the Harrods' logo.

'This morning—'

'I went into Airlie's to see if they had anything reasonable, but all their stock has become quite passé.'

'This morning, I was talking to George when—'

'George who?'

'Gardener George.'

'Mercer,' she corrected sharply.

He picked up the two bags and followed her inside. She went upstairs, he returned to the blue room. He finished his drink as she entered. She switched on the television. 'It's probably too late for *Neighbours*,' she said in tones of annoyance.

The picture formed on the screen and showed end credits. She changed channels. 'I'd like a vodka and tonic for a change. But not much vodka, not nearly as much gin as you'll have been drinking.'

He thought of explaining he'd been having Cinzano and soda, accepted he'd be wasting both time and breath. All she was interested in was projecting the image of a very light drinker. He left and went through to the butler's pantry, poured a generous tot of vodka, added a little tonic. When he returned, she was watching a cartoon. He held out the glass.

'Can't you put it down?'

He put the glass down on the small piecrust table. 'A detective called this morning. He was making enquiries concerning the fatal accident in Potters Road the week before last.'

Her face became drawn from shock. She drank eagerly.

'The police reckon the car which hit the woman was a silver Mercedes similar to yours.'

'Why bother us?' She tried, and failed, to speak casually.

'They want to examine your car.'

'Why?'

'To eliminate any possibility it was the one involved.'

'Didn't you tell them it wasn't?'

'Yes.'

'Then that's an end to it.'

'No.'

'Of course it is.'

'The detective is returning tomorrow morning at ten thirty to examine your car.'

'Ridiculous and insulting.'

'Insulting, or not, he'll be here.'

'You may not have had the gumption to send him packing, but I have.' She drained her glass, held it out. 'You can put a little more vodka in this time. I didn't mean you to make it quite so weak.'

He took her glass, but remained standing where he was. 'He will want to see your car, whatever you say.'

'I'll make it very plain I refuse.'

'That wouldn't be very tactful.'

'Since when has there been any need to be tactful to someone like him?'

'Sensible, if you prefer. If you refuse to cooperate, he's bound to assume you have reason for doing so. That means they'll impound your car and take it away for a very detailed examination.'

'Nonsense. This is England, not Russia.'

'There can be times where authority is concerned when only an initial touch of politeness marks the difference . . . I asked him what the police will be looking for. Signs of contact. Obviously that could be a broken headlight, paint patterned or flaked off, a dent.'

'Why bore me with all that?'

'Because there's a dent on the offside wheel arch of the Merc.'

'What are you suggesting?' she demanded shrilly.

'What caused that dent?'

'How should I know? Some little guttersnipe must have hit the car because it's so smart.'

'Anyone deciding to express angry jealousy is far more likely to have used the milled edge of a coin.'

'What does it matter?'

'Did you hit that woman?'

'You . . . you swine!' she shouted. 'Daring to accuse me!'

'Asking, not accusing.'

'You'll do anything to hurt me.'

'I'd never willingly do that . . . Portia, please, just tell me, did you hit that woman?'

'What have I done to have to suffer a husband who wants to believe his wife killed someone?'

'When she was hit, she was on the road you take when you return from Winifred's.'

'I told you, I wasn't at her place.'

'But you were.'

'Now you're trying to call me a liar. My God, I've had more than enough . . .'

'You were at her place that night and got tight.'

'I never have too much to drink.'

'When you returned here, you forgot to close the outside gates and left the Merc in the courtyard with the keys in the dash; when you came into the house, you were halfway to being legless.'

'I've never before realized just how vicious-minded you are. You're trying to get your own back on me, aren't you?'

'Of course not.'

'D'you think I don't know you resent me because I have all the money?'

'Can't you forget that and understand I'm trying to help you?'

'By accusing me of killing someone? A very strange kind of help!'

'By making you understand that if you did hit her, it has to be in your interests even at this late stage to confess to the police. They can't prove you were tight unless Winifred tells them that you did drink heavily at her place . . .'

'I wasn't there.'

'But you were. And there can be only one reason for denying it and that's to evade the obvious conclusion that on your way back here, you drove along Potters Road, that since you arrived back here at roughly a quarter past ten, you must have been in the vicinity of the accident at the time it took place . . .'

'How you're enjoying this! Trying to make up for all the years you've had to live with the shame of knowing that but for me you'd be poor. Who were you when we met? A failure. A down-and-out failure. So now you want to tell the police a filthy lie so that you can laugh at me . . .'

'Has it once occurred to you that a woman was killed?'

'It happens every day on the roads.'

'You still say you did not hit that woman?'

'Since it's true, of course I do.'

'Then you've no reason to fear the police knowing you were at Winifred's that night . . .'

'I wasn't,' she said furiously.

'And that you returned along Potters Road. Since there's a duty to help the police . . .'

'What a spineless hypocrite you are. Trying to conceal revenge under the name of duty . . . You'd better understand something.' Her words were coated in venom. 'If you try to get your own back by lying to the police, I'll see you're ruined. I own a lot of shares in Andrew & Sachs and Bert Fowler was a personal friend of my father. If I speak to him, you'll be out. At your age and without any qualifications, you'll never find another job. And you won't be living in this house on my money, that's for certain.'

He left the room.

He lay in bed and stared up at the ceiling, dimly visible because the moon was almost full and the curtains allowed some light to filter through. When one enjoyed the benefits of a civilized life, one owed a duty to honour those commitments which formed the building blocks of it – actively to support justice was one such commitment, to honour one's wife, another. By double-thought, he had been able to convince himself that Portia might not have been driving the car which had killed the woman; he could no longer do so. Drunk, she had driven so erratically she had hit the woman and then continued, careless whether the other was dead or would die unless help was called immediately. But she was his wife. So he was faced by two contradictory duties. Which did he honour? And did he possess the will to reach a decision without reference to her threats to send him back to the life he had escaped by marrying her?

Eleven

The PC walked along the row of terrace houses in Lowcoat Avenue until he came to No. 36. He knocked on the front door, which abutted directly onto the pavement, and when there was no response went on to No. 38. The door was opened by a woman whose appearance it would be generous to describe as blowsy. Many of his colleagues would have addressed her with ill-concealed contempt, but he had the generosity of mind never to judge by appearance. 'Sorry to bother you, Missus, but can you tell me if Carol Fowler still lives next door?'

She spoke challengingly. 'What's it to you?'

'Routine enquiries.'

She raised her cigarette to her mouth, drew on it, flicked the stub past him onto the pavement.

'So does she?'

'Can't say.'

'Not when you live next door?'

'That's right.'

'Not good neighbours, then?'

'Suppose you really say why you're asking?'

'She's been killed in a car accident.'

'Christ!' she exclaimed and stared at him, her face slack.

'So I need to know where her kid is and whether there are any relations who have to be told.'

After a while, she said: 'Never heard of any relations . . . What d'you know about her?' she asked, with sudden, sharp challenge.

'She was on the game.'

'No cause for spitting.'

'I've no intention of doing so.'

'Maybe that's right,' she said, as she studied him. 'Best come in.'

The front room was well furnished, but untidy. He stared at the framed print of Velázquez's *Water Seller of Seville* which hung at an angle and wondered how long it had been like that.

'D'you feel like a drink?'

'No, thanks.'

'I need one 'cause I liked her, in spite of everything, and it comes nasty to be told she's dead.'

She left, returned with a well-filled glass. As she sat on the settee, her body seemed to ebb downwards. 'I've always said, someone's got to do what she did or no woman would be safe. Had many a laugh when she told me about the things her clients wanted . . .'

He listened patiently.

'There's those what live round here who talk about her. I always say to 'em, don't look down on anyone or you'll look up and find someone what's staring down on you.'

'Very true.' He took the opportunity to direct the conversation. 'So where's her kid?'

'Norma's with Maisie, two roads down. I'd have had her, but Dad's not fond of kids,' she added sadly.

'Is she there now?'

'I suppose.'

'Will you give me the address?'

'Five, Bolton Terrace.'

'And Maisie's surname is . . . ?

She shook her head. 'Can't rightly say. Never known her as anything but Maisie.'

Ten minutes later, he made his way to Bolton Terrace. The houses here were set back from the pavement and whilst a few still had small front gardens, most had paved these areas for parking cars.

Maisie Anstey was small, sharp, and sparrow-like. 'She's staying here, sure, but right now she's three doors along playing with friends. She'll be as well looked after as if she was here,' she added quickly, as if he might believe Norma could be running wild.

'I've some very bad news for her.'

'What's that?' She began to fiddle with a ring on her finger.

'I'm afraid her mother's been killed in a car accident,' he said baldly, convinced that in the long run this was better than trying to break the news gently.

She stared unseeingly at the bricked-up fireplace. 'Dear God, the poor child! Now she's no one.'

He waited a while before he said: 'When you talk about "no one", does that mean there aren't any relatives?'

'There's probably some, but no saying where. All Carol ever said was she hated her family. Her father used to abuse her – know what I mean?'

'Unfortunately, yes.'

'And her mum wouldn't believe her and told her dad what she'd said and he roughed her up to teach her to keep quiet about it. So Carol cleared off and came south. She had some money she'd taken from her dad without his knowing, only that didn't last no time and . . . Well, she got mixed up with the wrong kind and ended up on the streets.' She stared at him to judge his reaction to what she'd just said.

'Life kicks some more than others.'

'She deserved better . . . Some years ago, she had Norma. Didn't know who the father was, of course, but loved the kid so much she talked about giving up the streets and finding a regular job. Never did. She made good money and it ain't easy to see that disappear . . . I was scared something terrible would happen to her; always

90

reading such things in the paper. I kept saying, get that job; maybe it won't pay well, but social will give you extra and you won't have someone wanting to do all sorts of dreadful things to you. Then she fell ill and I had to lend her a bob, or two, not that I'd many to spare. When she got better, she was offered a lot of money to go abroad. I told her, watch them foreigners, they ain't like us and some of the things they like doing . . . I'm not speaking 'em to a man. She wouldn't listen, said she'd make up all the money she'd lost and more through being ill. Asked me to look after Norma . . . If she hadn't gone abroad, this wouldn't of happened.'

'The accident occurred in this country,' he said quietly.

'Is that so? Thought from the way things were, her not coming back here, it was abroad . . . Doesn't change things, does it?'

'Not really. Where abroad did she go?'

'No idea. No, that's a bit of a lie. She told Norma it was Africa and she'd try to bring her back an elephant. The kid thought she meant a real one.'

'Does Norma know which part of Africa?'

'She said it was a town and I must show her where it was on a map. I tried to explain there's lots of towns in Africa, but I don't think she really understood . . . So what happens now to Norma?'

'I'll get in touch with social services and they'll let you know what their decision is.'

'Them!' she said, with contempt. 'So will it be them or me what has to tell her her mum's never returning home?'

'It'll surely be kinder if it's you.'

'For her, maybe, but not for me,' she replied grimly.

Tragedy – and crime was a tragedy – rippled ever outwards.

They finished breakfast just before ten. Frayne stacked the

tray and carried it through to the kitchen, put the dirty plates and cutlery into the dishwasher. Portia looked at her watch. 'I'm going out.'

'Have you forgotten the detective will be here at half past?'

'That's of no consequence to me.'

'Didn't you understand a word of what I said last night?'

'I'm not going to let some nasty little man dictate to me.'

'He'll dictate one hell of a lot more if you're not careful. Can't you see that if you're not here with your car, he'll view that as a sign of guilt?'

'I'm not responsible for his stupidity.'

'Where are you going?'

'To church.'

'You haven't been to church in years.'

'Is that any reason for not going this morning?'

'It's reason for thinking you're not going.'

'It's interesting to discover how eager you are to call me a liar,' she said angrily.

'I'm trying to make things easy for you. It's not the right time to assert yourself. Drive to church in the Audi and leave the Merc here for the detective to examine.'

'Haven't I just told you, I'm not having my life ordered by some grubby little policeman. And if you don't want to find yourself out in the cold, you'll make certain he doesn't try.'

'You make it sound as if I'll lie for you.'

'If it's necessary, I'm sure you will,' she said contemptuously. She took the car keys off the hook, walked past him and through the scullery to the back door.

Roach drove into the courtyard and stopped to the accompaniment of a mechanical groan from one of the rear brakes. The CID Fiesta had had a long, hard life; it should have been replaced at least a year before, but Accounts had deemed that financially impossible.

As he climbed out of the car, he noticed the empty garage. He presumed it was the Audi which was out. Frayne appeared from the house.

'Come on in,' he said.

'I'm in a bit of a rush, so if you don't mind, I'll just have a look at Mrs Frayne's Mercedes.'

'I'm sorry, but you can't.'

'Why's that?'

'My wife had a panicky phone call less than half an hour ago from her very aged aunt and had to rush off to discover if things are as bad as was made out. She asked me to say how sorry she is and does hope you'll understand.'

'Of course. But I'm sure you'll appreciate that this means I'll have to ask her to bring her car in to divisional HQ as soon as possible. Perhaps you'll get her to phone me and fix a time, preferably for tomorrow.'

'I have to confess that she rather objects to being ordered about.'

'Don't we all?'

'Isn't it sufficient for her to confirm she was not involved in the accident?'

'I'm sorry, no, it isn't . . . Is there any reason for her wishing us not to examine her car?'

'Of course not.'

'Then I look forward to hearing when will be convenient for it to be brought to the station.'

'The woman who was killed . . . According to the local paper, you don't know who she was.'

'We do now.'

'Was she married?'

'No.'

'Then things aren't quite as tragic as they might have been.'

'Depends how you rate them, Mr Frayne. She'd led a

rough life, but as I see things, that doesn't lessen the tragedy for her and certainly not for her young daughter.'

'When you say "rough", what does that mean?'

'We'll leave it at that, if you don't mind . . . I'll be off. And please make certain Mrs Frayne rings us to fix up everything. We far prefer to do things pleasantly.'

'The iron fist in the velvet glove?'

'You could put it that way.' Roach crossed to his car, started the engine, backed and turned, drove out on to the road.

Frayne stared at the small length of road seen through the gateway. A boy went past on a skateboard; a van with broken exhaust crackling, followed. Portia, Frayne thought, seemed to believe she could prevent the police examining the Mercedes by continued non-cooperation. She couldn't. And when the dent on the front offside wheelarch was examined, measured, and matched against the impact on the woman, there might be the proof that would turn suspicion into certainty. Should she be arrested, charged, and convicted, she would make certain his life was wrecked as hers was because that was her nature. Disaster lay ahead and there was no way of avoiding it. Nor should there be. She was guilty of causing death by drunken driving and he was guilty of . . . of selling his self-respect. Perhaps, in a twisted way, her persecution of him would restore a little of that. But at what cost? It was far easier to endure a harsh life if one had never endured an easy one. Could a partially restored self-respect ever balance a return to the degradation of near poverty?

He went back into the house and poured himself a large gin and tonic. In the blue room, he crossed to the window and looked out at the garden and its beauty was sharpened because soon it might be lost; he turned and looked at the richness of the furnishings and recalled the tiny room he had once, briefly, inhabited in which an orange box had been the table, a discarded mattress, the bed.

Roach had said that Carol Fowler had led a rough life, but that did not lessen the tragedy of her death. But might it not change the degree of culpability of killing her? It was a political nonsense to say that all men were born equal. They weren't. Some were born to rich parents, some to poor; some to loving parents, some to indifferent ones; some to be honest, others to be criminals. The police had not been able to identify Carol Fowler for several days after her death. Had she owned the car she was in, there would have been no such delay; had it been a friend's, had she hired it, there would have been only the briefest of delays. Then it had not been her car, nor had she had a right to be in it. 'A rough life' must mean a criminal one. Portia was diminished much less by Carol's death than she would have been by an innocent person's . . . He wished he could be certain he believed that.

The Mercedes drove into the courtyard, came to a stop. Portia climbed out and hurried through to the hall, called out. Frayne answered from the blue room and she went through. 'Well? What happened?'

'He was surprised to learn you weren't at home.'

'You told him I was at church?'

'I said you had to rush off to visit a sick aunt. That seemed to hold greater potential veracity, quite apart from denying him the chance to check the parked cars around the local churches.'

'He believed you?'

'Of course not. Detectives are carefully trained not to believe anyone.'

'Can't you talk seriously?'

He was gratified to see how nervous she was. 'He was convinced I was a liar and was lying because I knew you were lying about the accident. The upshot is, either you make an appointment to drive your car to the police station tomorrow where it will be examined or they'll come and collect it without your blessing.'

'I won't let them.'

'You can't stop them.'

'I'll hide the car.'

'Can't you appreciate the incriminating presumption that that sort of action will raise?'

'I did not hit the blasted woman.'

'They'll demand to know where you were that night. They'll question Winifred . . .'

'I wasn't at her place.'

'Portia, for God's sake, if we're to get anywhere, face facts. Convinced you were driving the car which hit and killed the woman, they'll unearth every movement of your evening. Far better to accept that and work out how to circumvent the conclusions they'll draw.'

She hesitated, crossed to one of the armchairs and sat. 'Circumvent?'

'Yes.'

'You mean, conceal certain things?'

'If possible.'

'You'll do that even though at the drop of a hat you'll deliver a sermon on the need for total honesty?'

'Sometimes there's the need, but not the will.'

'How you change when you're scared!'

'But you don't, which is the danger.'

She fidgeted with the arm of the chair. 'What can we do?'

'Admit you were at Winifred's, but make certain she gives you an alibi and swears you didn't have more than one drink. She'll do that for you, won't she?'

'I suppose so.'

He was disappointed by her lack of certainty. 'But if you and she—' He cut short the words.

'If she and I what?'

'Nothing,' he answered hastily. 'I'll drop something on the wheel arch of the Merc.'

'Why?'

'To cover up the dent already there with a bigger one. I'll use the sack of peat which George asked me to get from the garden centre and I've forgotten to tell him is on the floor of the garage. It's heavy enough and the pattern of the sacking will over-print anything that's already there.'

'What about the man who said it was my car he saw?'

'His description can't have been anything more than that it looked like an E series and was X registered. If the case ever reached court, a good counsel would make that evidence worthless.'

'Are you suggesting they could actually try me?'

'Unless we have more foresight than they have hindsight, it's very possible.'

'My God!'

Had she really thought she was insulated by her wealth? 'Phone Winifred . . . No, much better to go and see her. Explain how ridiculous the police are being, stress that the only way of stopping them in their tracks is for her to swear you were still in her house when the accident took place. Decide when you left her and I will arrange the time you arrived here . . .'

'Well?'

'It's not that simple as we've no idea when the police finally left Potters Road; it would be fatal to say you drove past when they were still there. You'll have to have come back along a different route. Why, when that would be longer?'

'I could say I returned via Meronstone.'

'Why would you have done that?'

'I wanted a quick word with Barbara.'

'She'll tell them she didn't see you.'

'She was in the Canaries at the time.'

'And you didn't know that?'

'I'd forgotten.'

'Wasn't it late to be calling on her?'

'She never goes to bed before midnight because she sleeps so badly.'

'And there are no close neighbours to deny any car drove in and, very soon afterwards, out . . . Why didn't you phone Barbara first to make certain it would be all right to call?'

'I only decided to do that after I left Winifred's and then I found the mobile's battery was flat so it wouldn't work.'

'We make a sharp team!' He drummed on the arm of the chair with his fingers. 'But are we missing anything?' After a while, he stood. 'I'll go and drop the sack of peat on your car.'

'If it's heavy, get Mercer to help you.'

'He's not here today. In any case, that would be somewhat counterproductive.'

'I'm not cut out to be a conspirator.'

And by the same token, he was? 'Suppose you drive off and talk to Winifred as soon as I've finished? The journey should add a touch of weathering. And find a solid reason why both of you should be certain what was the time when you left. Staying on to watch a TV programme would be as good as anything, wouldn't it?'

'I suppose so.'

'Right. I'll go on out to the garage.'

The peat had been teased out of a bale and loaded into a sack at the garden centre. After balancing the sack on his shoulders, he let it fall on the wing of the Mercedes. It produced a satisfying dent which completely obscured the smaller one that had been visible before.

Twelve

Roach entered Blundell's room. 'Mrs Frayne has just brought her Mercedes in.'

'And?'

'There's a dent in the offside wheel arch that would hold a pint of best bitter.'

'So we're getting somewhere at last.'

'Not necessarily.'

'Where's the problem?'

'Mrs Frayne said her husband was moving a sack of peat yesterday evening, slipped and dropped it on the car.'

'Did she manage to keep a straight face when she told you that? So what else does she have to say about the very "fortunate accident"?'

'Nothing. She refused to answer any questions and left in a huff and a taxi.'

'You just stood there and watched?'

'Short of arresting her, what else could I do?'

'Dredge up a little intelligence. You should have told her you'd be grateful if she'd help you – with her guilty conscience, she'd rush to help, hoping we'll think that's a sign of her innocence.'

'She wouldn't.'

'Why not?'

'You only have to meet her to know why.'

'That's an answer?'

'She's . . . She wouldn't give a damn what we think. She's class and people like us are supposed to knuckle.'

'What's that supposed to mean?'

'You know. In the old days, an inferior knuckled his forehead to a superior. Rather like lifting a hat to a lady.'

'Never done neither and bloody well never going to. So you just let her walk off without questioning her? She must have been laughing at you.'

'So if she wasn't talking, was I supposed to have arrested her even though there's only just enough evidence to suspect her?'

'I've told you what you should have done.'

'The rich live by different rules.'

'The law doesn't differentiate between rich and poor.'

'Tell that to an accused from the slums who can't afford a smart lawyer.'

'There are times when I really wonder if you're fitted out for this job.' Blundell came to his feet. 'We'll go down and look at the car, then I'll call in Vehicles while you drive out to the Fraynes' palace and, on bended knees, knuckle your bloody forehead as you beg them to allow you to have the sack of peat.'

'Mr Frayne's smart enough to have really used the sack to make the dent.'

'Sure. But the forensic boys can be a whole lot smarter than him. Underneath the bag marks, there'll be those of the dress Carol Fowler was wearing. And it'll be a cell bed for Duchess Frayne, instead of a half-toaster.'

'A what?'

'Are you that ignorant? The kind of bed the rich, what you respect so much, used to sleep in – wooden pillars and hangings all around so as no one could see what the Duke of Muck was getting up to with the tweeny.'

It would, Roach accepted, be inadvisable to suggest that what the other meant was half-tester.

Roach rang the bell, and after a while Enid opened the

door. She stared at him without speaking, her expression one of gloomy disapproval.

'Has Mrs Frayne returned?' he asked.

She nodded.

'Would you tell her I'd like a word with her, please. The name's Detective Constable Roach.'

She moved to one side, which he took to be an invitation to enter. Still without a word, she marched off. He shut the door. He wondered if he'd soon begin to feel superior if he lived in a large house surrounded by beautiful, valuable things? Was superiority a question of culture or nurture?

Portia came through a doorway and as she passed one of the two suits of armour, he visualized her wearing a third one.

She came to a stop some twelve feet from him.

Was she taking care to keep outside the contamination zone?

'This,' she said, her voice ice-laden, 'has become persecution.'

'I assure you . . .' he began.

'I am uninterested in worthless assurances. Over the course of several days, you have interrupted the lives of both my husband and me by asking impertinent questions. Today, I was for some ridiculous reason compelled to drive my car to the police station and leave it with you. I had to hire a taxi to return. Now, you are here yet again. The only words to describe such behaviour are, arrant persecution.'

'We do have to make enquiries . . .'

'Not when there is no justification for them.'

'Our justification is that a young woman was killed by a hit-and-run motorist.'

'How can that be of any account to me?'

'You feel no concern over her death?'

'That question is highly impertinent.'

Because she might well make an official complaint, he was advised to cover himself. 'I'm sorry if you should think that; it certainly wasn't meant to be in any way impertinent.'

She ignored his apology.

'I'd like, if I may, to see the sack of peat your husband accidentally dropped on your car.'

'Why?'

'It may well help in our investigation.'

'How?'

'By making certain it could not have been your car which struck and killed the victim.'

'It is an insult to suggest it could be.'

'Will you please show me the sack?'

'The gardener can do that.'

He clearly had been guilty of a serious social gaffe. He should have realized that a woman in her position would leave it to another to carry out his request. 'Where will I find him?'

'Would you expect to do so in the laundry?' She turned, crossed the hall and left through the doorway by which she had entered.

He opened the front door and went outside, round the house to the back garden. Mercer was edging the lawn with an electric cutter. 'Hullo, there.'

Mercer worked on for half a minute before he turned the machine off.

'Local CID. Mrs Frayne said to ask you to show me the sack of peat that Mr Frayne dropped on her car . . . I'll bet she had something to say about that!'

Mercer hawked and spat.

'From the sound of her, she's a bit of a Tartar?'

Mercer stared at nothing in particular.

'You've a lovely garden here. Must take a lot of work.'

'There's little done easy that's worthwhile.'

That sounded as if it had started life in an Xmas cracker. 'So where is this sack?'

'In the coach house.'

'And where's that?'

'Where it's always been.'

'Then suppose you lead me to it before it decides to move.'

They crossed the lawn to the door between the corner of the house and the brick wall which separated the garden from the courtyard.

'You've been here before,' Mercer said, as he opened the door.

'That's right.'

He went through the doorway. 'Something up?' he asked, curiosity overcoming his reserve.

'Just routine,' Roach answered, as he followed through into the courtyard.

'Funny sort of routine, you wanting to see the sack what he dropped on the car.'

'Our job's like that. Spend half our lives doing things which don't seem to make sense.'

'Lucky to be able to waste the time.' He went over to the left-hand garage, walking with the careful stride of someone who was on his feet most of the day. He pressed the right-hand button on the control panel and the door began to rise and slide inwards. 'Orders is for the door to be shut when the car's not there. Waste of electricity, seeing as it has to be opened when the car returns.'

A man who watched the kilowatts.

He pointed.

Roach went over to the rough woven sack that was almost full. He lifted it. 'There's a fair weight in it.'

'So there should be, considering what it costs.'

He rested the sack on the ground. 'I'll be taking this with me.'

'Oh, aye! Why?'

'Routine.'

'There's some strange routines you blokes gets up to. Something is up, ain't it?'

'If there is, no one's told me about it. Maybe the soil in the superintendent's garden needs a bit of something to pep it up.'

'If there's any missing when it comes back, she'll have something to say.'

'Only joking. But if you've a set of scales, we'll weigh the lot and make a note on the receipt I'll be giving you. That should keep her quiet.'

'Nothing won't manage that.'

'Always has the last word, does she?'

'And the first.'

'What about Mr Frayne?'

'Different. When he talks, it ain't always giving orders or complaining.'

'Must make a pleasant change . . . So I'll give you a receipt for the sack, listing a quantity of peat and hope she doesn't complain a handful's missing when you get it back.' Roach wrote out a receipt and handed it to Mercer. As he lifted the sack, he said: 'I wouldn't want to heft this all the way back to the station.'

'I'd like to see how far you'd get!'

Obviously, in Mercer's judgement, no distance at all. He was inclined to agree.

Frayne was recording a letter when the internal phone buzzed. He stopped the tape, lifted the receiver.

'Mrs Frayne is on the line,' Sandra said.

'Put her through, please.'

'You're not forgetting the meeting with Mr Ash?'

'I'm doing my best to try to.'

'It'll take you a good twenty minutes to get to his place and there's only half an hour to go.'

'I'll not spend long chatting to my wife.'

'What husband would?' She cut the connection.

He replaced that receiver, lifted the second one.

'The detective's just been,' Portia said.

104

'How did things go?'

'He wanted to look at the sack and had the insolence to expect me to show it to him. I told him to speak to Mercer.'

He mentally sighed. It was not difficult to imagine her manner when she'd said that – it would have helped if only she could for once have appeared friendly. A man who felt he had reason to be resentful would be that little more eager to uncover something incriminating. 'Did he take the sack when he left?'

'Mercer came and handed me the receipt and wanted to know if it was all right.'

'How did you answer?'

'Told him it was.'

'Did you give him some sort of explanation for what was going on?'

'Of course not. That's none of his business.'

'Was he very curious?'

'How does one tell what he is? He's probably never wondered about anything in his life.'

'Did the detective ask him if he'd seen a dent on the wheel arch before I dropped the sack on it?'

'I've no idea. I don't spend my time chatting to the servants.'

'I'll have to try to find out without raising his curiosity any higher. His noticing the first dent is something I didn't think of . . . Still, with any luck, he won't have done so. You always park bonnet in, so there's never much light on the front end of the car; I'm pretty certain it would have needed good light to make it out . . . Has Winifred been in touch with you?'

'Why should she have been?'

'She could have developed doubts about supporting your story to the police and want to talk things over with you.'

'I made certain she wouldn't.'

'How?'

'By giving her a cheque for a thousand.'

'You what?'

'Gave her a thousand pounds.'

'My God! You . . .' He checked the words, spoke more calmly. 'Do you think that was wise?'

'She's so hard up, it'll be a fortune to her.'

'But surely it would have been better . . .'

'Why do you have to criticize everything I do?'

Because she was so self-centred, she seemed incapable of appreciating other people's emotions. 'I'm not criticizing, just evaluating.'

'Then do that less argumentatively. I think we must complain that the police are persecuting us.'

'Right now, it would be much more sensible not to do anything to antagonize them.'

Which conclusion naturally antagonized her.

'We can confirm the dent on the Mercedes offside wheel arch was caused by the sack of peat,' Vehicles reported at 1750 hours on Friday.

'No one ever thought different,' Blundell said. 'What we're interested in—'

'Wouldn't like to wait for the rest of it, would you?'

The men in Vehicles acted like they were all inspectors. 'I'm waiting and waiting and pretty soon I'll disappear behind the cobwebs.'

'That'll be OK by us . . . According to the metallurgical experts, the deformation of the metal suggests it may have been subjected to two separate forces, striking at different angles. At one point beneath the imprint of the sack there is what could be a previous imprint that corresponds to the marks one would expect if the victim's dress had been pressed against it.'

'Then you'll go into court and say that the car did strike the woman and later the sack of peat was dropped on it, almost certainly to try to obliterate the marks of the first impact?'

'You're in the next race. Listen to the mays and the mights. What I've said is what we're reasonably certain is fact. Put us in court and it'll be no stronger than perhaps it was like that.'

'Then a sharp counsel would make what we allege seem as likely as a four-headed duck?'

'Precisely.'

'Why can't you blokes ever make up your minds?'

'Life's too short.'

Blundell went along to the DI's room. 'Just had Vehicles on the blower, sir, with a report on the Frayne Mercedes. They reckon there were two impacts and the first bears marks likely from the woman's dress. But they can't be sufficiently positive to provide a good case in court.'

'Typical! Then when we question the wife, we'll just have to make out we've such a damning case against her, honesty is the best policy.'

Thirteen

Howes would never have admitted it, but he felt out of place in Bell's House. He had been born into what, in the days before euphemistic correctness, had been known as a lower middle-class home, had married when young, and he and his wife had worked hard yet never made more than just enough to house, clothe, and feed what, until he'd braved himself to suffer a vasectomy, had been an ever-growing family. When he looked down at the large carpet in the centre of the blue room – Isfahan Seirafian hunting design, not that he knew that – he saw not the stylized scene of men on horseback, armed with swords, bows and arrows, or lances, attacking or being attacked by both realistic and mythical animals, but untold thousands of pounds; to be able to leave such wealth invested in beauty, not living, was a luxury which both offended him and engendered jealousy.

'Naturally we can understand that you have to make enquiries—' Frayne began.

Portia interrupted him. 'But not that we should suffer this continuing persecution.'

She held her solid jaw well forward and Howes, with a rare flash of imagination, thought of the battering ram on the bows of a Venetian galley. 'Mrs Frayne, I can assure you . . .'

'As I told the young man who has continually been bothering us, we are uninterested in worthless assurances.'

Frayne hurried to soothe ruffled feelings. 'Obviously,

we find the visits a little disturbing, but if we can help in any way, we most certainly will.'

'And as a matter of fact, you can,' Howes said.

'Then you'll no doubt explain how.'

'An eye-witness saw the car which killed Carol Fowler and he described it as a silver Mercedes, X registered, precisely similar in appearance to the one owned by someone he named. We had a list drawn up of all comparable cars owned in the county and Mrs Frayne's was one of these. In this kind of case, our first task is to eliminate all cars which could not possibly have been involved, which is why we originally contacted Mrs Frayne. Unfortunately, she was unwilling to have her car examined . . .'

'Since I have not been involved in any accident, I saw no reason why it should be,' she snapped.

'Most people, Mrs Frayne, would—'

'I have always hoped I am of sufficient intelligence not to be compared to the herd.'

If he'd had a pair of antlers, he knew exactly where he'd aim them. He looked at Bullard, hoping for some verbal support, but the detective sergeant was carefully staring down at the small tape recorder he held. 'As I was about to say, Mrs Frayne, most people understand that to deny such a request must be to raise the question of why it has been made.'

'The inspector has quite a point, dear,' Frayne said. 'After all, if it is incorrectly assumed one might be responsible for committing a crime, the natural reaction is to deny the possibility.'

'Which I did.'

'Of course. But had you agreed to your car's being examined, your denial would have been incontrovertibly corroborated.' He turned to Howes. 'My wife has, if I can put it like this, a developed sense of property. That's why she refused the request – she saw it as a challenge to her possession. You'll understand, I hope?'

Howes had not heard much that was less comprehensible. 'But when we made a second request . . .'

'Demand,' she snapped.

'We had to examine your car, Mrs Frayne, if we were to eliminate it from our investigation. In the end, of course, you agreed to drive it to divisional HQ. From there, we had it transported – on a low-loader so that there could be no question of any damage caused by driving it on the open roads – to county HQ, where experts examined it. We're here because of what they discovered.'

'They—'

Frayne immediately interrupted her. 'From the way you speak, Inspector, it seems as if the experts claim to have found something they consider important?'

'Yes, they do.'

'Allegedly connecting my wife's car with the accident?'

'That is so.'

'Then they are mistaken.'

'I have to tell you, they very seldom make mistakes.'

'This is clearly one occasion when they have.'

'The large dent in the offside front wheelarch of Mrs Frayne's car was definitely caused by the sack of peat.'

'Which is what you were told.'

'Quite. But the distortion of the metal points to the fact it was subjected to two forces, coming from slightly different directions.'

'The corner of the bottom of the bag hit the car. That meant more than one angle of sack was presented.'

'One force was of a different nature from the other.'

'That can be positively determined?'

'I gather so.'

'I wonder if an independent metallurgical expert would agree?'

'Not for me to comment on that . . . Naturally, there was the imprint of the sack on the paintwork. But underneath this, they discovered a second imprint which corresponds with the pattern of the dress the victim was wearing.'

'You—' Portia began before her husband once again hurriedly interrupted her.

'Let me understand exactly what you are now saying. Are you alleging it was my wife's car which struck the very unfortunate woman and the grounds for that claim are that on the paintwork is the imprint of the dress she was wearing?'

'That is correct.'

'Is this second imprint so very clear, despite being underneath the sack's imprint, that the experts are positive?'

Howes hesitated. To answer in the affirmative might persuade them that they had nothing to gain by continuing denials, but Frayne gave the impression of a man who would not easily fold. If, in court, he was challenged by the defence and asked whether he had told the Fraynes there was proof positive when he must have known there was not, he would expose himself as a liar; juries could be so naively irrational that if it were shown a senior investigating officer had lied on one point, they would fail to understand it had been a tactical move and they would accept the defence's assertion that a man who lied on one point, would lie on many. 'Not quite,' he finally answered.

'What exactly does that mean?'

'It is a question of degree of legal proof.'

'Is that a roundabout way of saying they're presuming, without sufficient evidence, to make such a presumption?'

'They judge the mark was made by the victim's dress, but in court they would be unable to swear that, beyond any doubt, it was. They can offer a degree of probability, not certainty.'

'Which makes it far from convincing evidence.'

'Confirmatory evidence can become convincing when allied to other evidence. Which is why I must now ask Mrs Frayne certain questions.'

'You are arresting her?'

'No.'

'She is entitled to have a solicitor present when she answers your questions?'

'Of course.'

'Since it must be very much in the interests of her innocence to have that protection, she will answer nothing until she does.'

Howes turned to Portia. 'You wish a solicitor to be present when I question you?'

'My husband has just told you so.'

'Then we will arrange a time for you to come to divisional headquarters.'

'The meeting will be at her solicitor's office,' Frayne corrected.

Ten minutes later, Howes and Blundell left the house and crossed the courtyard to their car. As Blundell started the engine, he said: 'Seems it was a bit too difficult to persuade 'em that honesty is the best policy.'

'Because you were as much use as a punctured balloon,' Howes said angrily.

The rest of the drive was made in silence.

Fourteen

C lifford was a model family solicitor; not tall, not short, not thin, not fat, a middle-aged man of unremarkable appearance who did not wear his sharp intelligence on his sleeve. 'Since we are ready, Inspector, perhaps you'd like to ask Mrs Frayne the questions you wish to put to her?'

The office was large and there was plenty of room for the four comfortable chairs, in front of the antique partners desk, on which the Fraynes, Howes, and Roach sat. Facing west, sunlight came through the wide single window and highlighted the rows of textbooks on the shelving behind the desk. Howes, on the right-hand chair, cleared his throat, conscious of the need not to give the lawyer an inch which he'd promptly turn into a yard. 'Mrs Frayne, you own a silver-coloured Mercedes . . .'

'There's no dispute as to that,' Clifford said.

Of course there wasn't. The other was merely trying to put him off his stride. 'Our investigation into the death of Carol Fowler has shown that it was a silver-coloured X-registered Mercedes, model E three-twenty, which struck her on the eighth of this month and we have reason to believe it may have been your car which was involved.'

'My client denies the allegation, completely and absolutely,' Clifford said.

'There is evidence which seems to identify your client's car as the one in question.'

'Either the evidence is incorrect, or the wrong conclusions are being drawn from it.'

Lawyers could make a meal out of saying hullo. 'Was it your car, Mrs Frayne, that knocked Carol Fowler down?'

'No.'

So short an answer from a woman who liked to express her aggressive feelings told Howes she had been well coached. 'Can you tell me where you were on the eighth, a Tuesday?'

'I was at home in the morning; I went out in the late afternoon.'

'When did you return home?'

'Some time around a quarter past eleven.'

'Did you drive home in your Mercedes?'

'Yes.'

'Where had you been?'

'At a friend's house.'

'May I have your friend's name?'

'Miss Leston.'

'Were you in her house all evening?'

'Yes.'

'Where does Miss Leston live?'

'High Barnfield.'

'You were at her home in High Barnfield on the evening of the eighth of this month?'

'Mrs Frayne has already told you so,' Clifford said.

'Indeed.' It was always pleasant to get someone on the run; trebly pleasant when that someone was this woman. 'Mrs Frayne, what is the shortest route between High Barnfield and Fretstone?'

'I've no idea.'

'Let me put it another way. When you drive to Miss Leston's home, or return from there, do you pass through the village of Wrathware?'

'Usually.'

'Then you take the shortest route.'

'Opinion rather than fact at this stage,' Clifford said.

And now you're going to get some fact, Howes silently

114

said. 'Mrs Frayne, if you pass through Wrathware on returning from High Barnfield, you must travel along Potters Road.'

'Really.'

'Did you take that route home on the eighth?'

'No.'

'Why not?'

'Mrs Frayne is entitled to drive home along any route she chooses,' Clifford said.

'Quite. But if one normally takes one route, there is usually a reason why one chooses another, especially if it is longer.'

'Which may be no more than the wish for a change.'

'Mrs Frayne, what was your reason for returning home by a different route from the one you normally take?'

'I wanted to have a word with a friend.'

'May I have her name?'

'I'm not—' she began angrily.

'Mrs Frayne,' Clifford said quietly, 'there can be no objection to providing this information.'

She obviously disagreed, but said: 'Mrs Barbara Fenton.'

'Where does Mrs Fenton live?'

'On the outskirts of Meronstone.'

'Wasn't it rather late at night to call on her?'

'She never goes to bed before midnight.'

'She will be able to confirm that you called on her?'

'No.'

'Why is that?'

'She was away on holiday.'

'You did not know this?'

'Would I have gone to her house if I had not for-gotten?'

'Can we go back in time to when you left Miss Leston's house. What time was that?'

'Half-past ten.'

'You can be certain?'

'Yes.'

'Why is that?'

'Because I am.'

'Perhaps there is some occurrence that makes you so certain?' Clifford suggested.

'We were watching the news and that came to an end.'

'Then you were watching BBC One?'

'I'd prefer Mrs Frayne to supply the answers,' Howes said.

'Merely trying to assist,' Clifford replied sweetly.

'You left at ten thirty and returned home via Meronstone?' Howes couldn't quite conceal his angry irritation.

'Inspector,' Clifford said, 'this must be quite an ordeal for Mrs Frayne and therefore it surely would be better if the same questions are not repeatedly asked?'

'I like to be quite certain that I have the facts correctly . . . One last thing, Mrs Frayne. Would you please give me Miss Leston's address?'

'Littlebourne, Chivers Road.'

'And that is in High Barnfield?'

'Yes.'

'Is that all?' Clifford asked.

Hadn't he just said so? 'Yes, thank you.'

'You agree that you have received full cooperation from my client?'

Apart from her lying. 'She has answered my questions.' Howes stood; Roach did the same. 'Your evidence, Mrs Frayne, will help us take our investigations forward.' As he left the room, he hoped his last remark would make them feel as if they'd swallowed some bad fish.

Outside the nineteenth-century building, Roach said: 'I never had time for breakfast.'

'I'm not interested in your problems.'

'But it's like this, sir, I feel as if a rat were gnawing at my guts. Is there any chance of stopping off for a coffee and a doughnut at the café just around the corner – wouldn't take five minutes?'

'They'll remain upstairs for a while because the mouthpiece will want to assure 'em it's all thanks to his cleverness that they're now in the clear. So we're driving straight off to High Barnfield to get there before those two return home and phone the Leston woman to make certain she says the right things.'

Frayne said: 'Do you think it'll be the end of it despite his parting shot?'

'That was just an expression of frustration,' Clifford replied.

'Then they'll stop harassing us now?' Portia asked.

Clifford leaned forward and rested his arms on the desk. 'They'll question your friend, Miss Leston, of course, and ask her to confirm the time you left her home. Once she does that, they can have no valid reason to bother you again.'

'Can you be that certain?' Frayne said.

'The inspector is a plodder, but not a fool. So when it has to be obvious that Mrs Frayne could not have been driving along Potters Road at the relevant time, he will accept the fact that despite those dubious pieces of evidence, there is absolutely no point in continuing to believe in the possibility that it was her car which hit the unfortunate woman.' He paused briefly, then continued: 'It is unfortunate that you have been unnecessarily embroiled in this affair, but for you, any connection with it is now at an end.'

'Bit of a difference,' Roach said, as he braked the car to a halt.

'What is?' Howes asked, his mind having been back in the solicitor's office.

'Finding she lives in a bungalow like this. Hardly to be expected.'

'Why not?'

'I'd have bet she lived in somewhere as grand as the Fraynes. After all, the Lord of the Manor isn't usually friendly with the dustman.'

'I've heard Conservatives talk more sense than you.'

Roach climbed out onto the pavement, locked the driving door – nothing could provoke such cruel humour as a policeman's having his car stolen – and led the way along the imitation crazy-paving path which was breaking up. The front door needed repainting. He rang the bell.

'Leave me to do the talking,' Howes said.

'With pleasure, sir.'

'Enough of that!'

The inspector was a man of few moods, Roach thought. When they'd left the solicitor's office, his manner had been sour, now it was sourer.

Winifred opened the door, visually examined them, said: 'Yes?' in a challenging tone.

'Detective Inspector Howes and Detective Constable Roach, local CID,' Howes answered.

'Well?'

Her dishevelled appearance would have suggested very low self-esteem had her attitude not proclaimed the opposite. 'Sorry to bother you, Miss Leston, but we'd like a word if that's convenient?'

'And if it isn't?'

'The matter is important.'

'To whom?'

'To justice.'

'When a policeman starts talking about justice, it's obvious there's been some sort of balls-up.'

Howes was sufficiently old-fashioned to be shocked by her choice of words. Crudity from a man was unwelcome, from a woman, unpardonable.

'Do you intend to spend the rest of the day just standing here?'

118

They entered a tiny hall that was untidy; they went from there into a small sitting room that was even more untidy. A snuffling Pekinese yapped at them until she shouted at it to shut up. She sat and the dog jumped onto her lap.

Howes waited for an invitation to sit; none came. When Roach settled on the settee, he decided it was each man for himself, collected up a pile of magazines from the second armchair, put them on an occasional table which lacked half its raised beaded edge. The chair smelt of dog. He sat. 'Miss Leston, there was a fatal accident on the eighth of this month in Potters Road. A car had stopped because of a puncture . . .'

'There's no need for all that waffle. I saw the report in the local rag.'

Had anyone thought to tell her that manners makyth woman as well as man? 'An oncoming car came round the corner and hit the woman who was standing on the off side of the first car and she suffered fatal injuries; the car did not stop. Naturally, we are trying to identify the driven . . .'

'Why bother me?'

'We have a list of cars which match the description of the car involved and are working to eliminate all those which were not concerned with the incident.'

'For the first two weeks of this month, my car was at the garage. The sodding thing's always breaking down.'

He concealed his distaste for this further crudity. Roach would probably claim her father had been either a duke or a dustman. 'Our concern is not with your car, Miss Leston, but with one belonging to a friend of yours.'

'Then what's the good of bothering me?'

'I'm sure you'll be able to help . . .'

'Leave me to decide that.'

'I understand Mrs Frayne visited you here on the eighth?'

'So?'

'Perhaps you'll confirm when she arrived?'

'The afternoon.'

'About when?'

'In time for coffee.'

'And when did she leave?'

She suddenly stood. 'Percy needs a shit,' she said and carried the dog out of the room.

Howes noticed Roach was smiling. 'Is something amusing you?' he demanded roughly.

Roach stopped smiling.

Winifred returned. 'I've left him in the kitchen because his back end needs cleaning up. Have you ever wondered what happened when we weren't around to do it for them?'

Howes was not going to answer a question like that. 'Miss Leston, can you say when Mrs Frayne drove away from here on the evening of the eighth?'

It took her time to settle on the chair. Even then, it was several seconds before she said: 'I don't wear a watch.'

'You wouldn't like to judge what the time was?'

'No.'

'Mrs Frayne says you watched the ten o'clock news. Would you agree?'

'Why ask me if she's told you?'

'She left when the news finished. That would make the time ten thirty, or ten thirty-five.'

She said nothing.

'Is that how you remember things?'

'Probably.'

'It would help us if you could be more definite.'

'I don't spend my time clock-watching.'

'You cannot confirm what she has told us?'

'Or deny it.'

'During the course of the evening, did you and Mrs Frayne have a drink?'

'Naturally.'

'What did you both have?'

'Margaritas.'

'I'm not certain exactly what that is.'

'Hardly surprising.'

Because he had seldom so immediately disliked anyone, Howes chose to believe her two words were a social insult. 'How many drinks did Mrs Frayne have during the course of the evening?'

'I've no idea.'

'More than one?'

'No idea means I don't bloody well remember.'

'I suspect that if she had had only one, you would remember. Perhaps she had several?'

'You're beginning to irritate me.'

'Would you agree—'

She stood. 'You can go.'

'I haven't finished—'

'You have. So bugger off.'

They left.

As Roach drove away from the pavement, Howes said: 'My God, I thought her kind had been buried years ago. Using language that would make a navvy feel at home, yet speaking as if she was wearing a tiara.'

'Maybe she did wear one once,' Roach said. 'But life's been really tough and reduced her to subsistence level.'

'What level? She maybe lives and looks like a down-and-out, but she's got the bungalow, runs a car, obviously isn't starving, and drinks some goddamn awful mixture by the gallon.'

'In her eyes, it's likely subsistence level. Which would explain her bitter resentment.'

'At having the likes of me daring to question her?'

'Some of that.' Roach slowed to turn into a corner. 'But also resentment against Mrs Frayne.'

'The two obviously spent the afternoon and evening together boozing and you're trying to say they disliked each other?'

'I'm talking about Miss Leston. She wouldn't have paraded her feelings, probably pays her not to. But they could have been bubbling away for a long time.'

'Why should they?'

'I'd guess Miss Leston feels she's living at a very low level when she's with Mrs Frayne, who oozes money. Like as not, Mrs Frayne's parents were a long way downmarket of Miss Leston's and that would add fuel to the resentment.' He tucked the car more tightly to the side to give an oncoming heavy goods vehicle as much room as possible. 'I had the impression that when you asked what time Mrs Frayne left that evening, she wasn't certain how to answer which is why she said the dog needed out – to give her time to make up her mind.'

'If a dog wants out, you kick it out before it mucks on the carpet.'

'But did it? It was sitting quietly on her lap before she hurried it out of the room. If it had really been in a hurry, wouldn't it have jumped down from her lap and rushed over to the door?'

'I wouldn't know. Can't stand dogs because of the stink . . . Why wasn't she certain how she was going to answer?'

'Perhaps something's happened recently to increase her resentment to the point where she wanted to betray Mrs Frayne to us, yet couldn't quite bring herself to do so; that's why she made out she couldn't remember definite times, or anything much.'

'What's the something?'

'I don't know.'

'And there was me beginning to think you were omniscient!'

'But I can guess.'

'So guess.'

'Mrs Frayne offered her a small fortune to lie. She accepted the money because she needed it, but was so humiliated by her need, so despising herself because she succumbed to the temptation, that when it came to the point she wouldn't give us a direct answer because that allowed her to salve her conscience by assuring herself she didn't actually lie to us. There is one thing, though, I can't work out.'

'You surprise me.'

Roach became silent.

After a while, Howes said sharply: 'Well, what is it that escapes your brilliant psychological analysis?'

'Why is Mrs Frayne so friendly with her?'

'Why not?'

'Mrs Frayne's the kind of woman who patronizes; patronize Miss Leston and normally you'd be told where to go and exactly what to do when you got there, all in very basic language. So why should they get along like good friends? Could be, they're a couple of lezzies.'

'Sergeant Blundell told me not so long ago that you had an active imagination; I'd call that the greatest understatement of the century.'

Fifteen

As Frayne opened the wooden front gate, he noticed more paint had flaked off it. Several months ago he had suggested he should repaint it; Francesca had sharply refused the offer and for a while her attitude had remained frosty. He was convinced she had thought he was trying to ease himself into her life by making himself indispensable. He hadn't. At least, that was what he assured himself. Their relationship – she would probably deny there was one – was made for misunderstanding.

He walked along the brick path to the small porch, opened the outer door, rang the bell to the side of the inner, glass door. Francesca stepped out of the sitting room into the hall. She was wearing a dress that, ridiculously, made him think of Maria on top of the mountain, flinging wide her arms and singing. She opened the inner door.

'Am I welcome?' he asked.

'To be frank, not really.'

'Then I'll say goodbye as well as hullo.'

'Since you're here, you might as well come on in.'

He stepped into the hall with its steeply sloping ceiling. 'Is it me or life that's at fault?'

She spoke in a dull voice. 'Bill's walking again; dressed and fed himself yesterday morning. When I visited him, he kept asking me when I was going to bring him home. And I had to say . . . The look on his face when I told him I just couldn't cope. I wish to God he didn't have these remissions . . . You're listening to a bitch. Angry

124

because her husband temporarily returns to the world; angry because he isn't the cabbage he was . . .' She turned away. 'Sorry,' she said in a muffled voice.

'For what?'

'Breaking down.'

'Much better that than to keep on bottling up everything.'

'Perhaps . . . Would you like a drink?'

'I'd not refuse a gin and tonic.'

'Go on through. The booze is still in the kitchen with the shopping so I'll get it.'

'I should have brought a bottle.'

'Like hell you should! When I can't afford to provide the drinks, I don't offer them.'

She used her independence as a shield. He entered the sitting room and sat. He stared through the window at the two Bramley trees that were in view. His mother had made pies with apples whose names he could not now remember; they had tasted like ambrosia. In their two-acre orchard, there had been four or five varieties of apples which were now virtually lost because supermarkets demanded uniformity at the cost of flavour. In addition to apples, there had been pears, plums, and cherries. One of the farmhands had devised a machine for scaring the birds off the ripening cherries; it had terrified the family, not the birds . . .

'Miles away?' she asked, as she stepped into the room, a glass in each hand.

'Years away.'

'Never go back. I've had to learn the absolute wisdom of that.' She handed him a glass, crossed to the settee and settled on it, legs tucked under herself. 'The trouble is, we remember the good parts and forget the bad and that makes the present seem ten times worse . . . Enough of my moans. What's brought you here?'

'You.'

'Please don't.'

'I didn't mean that as you obviously think I did.'

'Correct me.' She drank.

'I came here . . .' He stopped.

'You came here?'

'Looking for sympathy. Which makes me a creep because my problems disappear when compared to yours.'

'Mine are insoluble. If yours aren't, maybe I can offer the sympathy you need.'

'Want would be a better word. Need might allow I deserve some sympathy.'

'Dick, either tell me straightforwardly what's wrong or we can talk about something neutral.'

He looked down at his glass, slowly turned it round in his hand. 'Have you ever hated yourself?'

'Often.'

'But never because you've looked into a mirror and recognized that what you saw was rotten.'

'I hope I've always been able to see a little that's worthwhile.'

'I can't.'

'Why not?'

He drank, lowered the glass, resumed turning it. 'You know my parents were quite wealthy before they ran into bad times?'

'You did mention that once.'

'When they died, I found I was suddenly virtually penniless. I was at university, so I applied for a grant and that was turned down. Someone with backbone would have found a way of making enough money to fund himself until he had the degree, I gave up on the excuse that there was no point since I was damned by fate. I decided to make the worst of everything. I became mixed up with layabouts, druggies, criminals . . .'

'Are you sure you want to tell me all this?'

'If I don't, you'll not be able to understand what follows.

Three of us decided to break into a house belonging to an old man who reputedly owned a fortune in antique silver. There weren't supposed to be any alarms, but that proved to be faulty information; added to which, there was a dog the size of a pony. We took to our heels, but Mick fell and injured himself while trying to clamber over a wall. So did we go to help him? We got the hell out of it while we still could.

'Mick would probably have gained a lighter sentence by naming the two of us, but although we'd betrayed him, he refused to betray us and the police never did identify us . . . He made me finally start thinking. If he could honour his code, I had to honour the one I should have observed. I saw myself using the example of his loyalty to redeem my disloyalty. The trouble was, redemption hurt. Without qualifications or experience, I had a succession of mindless, ill-paid jobs and life was very grey. Then I made contact with a relative from the past and through him, Portia. Know what attracted me to her? Her wealthy father. Impoverished dukes used to find American heiresses irresistible. Probably they still would if any heiress were stupid enough to give them the chance. It was a marriage of convenience on both sides.'

'Why on hers?'

'My attraction for her was as warped as hers for me. She wanted a married name because she was in increasing danger of remaining a spinster while all her friends and acquaintances achieved husbands – in her group, husbands were still a far better accessory than a live-in boyfriend. Her husband had to have a background that would help overcome hers, and to be in a position, or rather to lack one, that would let her dictate the course of the relationship from the beginning.'

'And has she?'

'It's the lack of money, not the love of money, which

is the root of all evil . . . I've since lied and committed a betrayal far worse than that previous one.'

'Who have you betrayed this time?'

'A concept, not a person. One I used to assure myself I'd honour throughout my life.'

'What is that?'

'Justice.'

There was a long silence.

'Another drink?' she finally asked.

'No, thanks.'

'Self-denial might help the ego?'

He looked at her with uneasy surprise.

'You don't think I haven't been there?' She moved her legs, stood, crossed to where he sat. 'Give me your glass.'

He handed it to her. When she returned, she settled once more on the settee. 'Maybe you set your standards too high.'

'Honouring justice and loyalty is too ambitious?'

'Circumstances can make it so.' She drank. 'I've wished Bill dead many times.'

'To save him the distress of going on living.'

'We had a traditional marriage – for better, for worse.'

'You've wished him the greatest gift life could now give him – death. Where's the disloyalty in that?'

'If only I could see it quite so straightforwardly . . . It's crazy. You came here for sympathy and ended up having to hold my hand.'

'Only after you'd given me all I needed.'

'How?'

'By accepting what I've told you and not being out-raged by it.'

Ten minutes later, he said: 'I guess I'd better start moving.'

'Do you have to return home now?'

'No.'

'Then stay.'

He did not make the mistake of hoping her invitation might extend to her bedroom.

The first of September brought heavy clouds, a cool wind, and the forecast of rain. Summer was preparing to leave.

Howes read the report for the second time. He stood, went round the desk, into the passage, and along to the next room. 'The CPS report is in,' he said.

'What's the verdict, sir?' Blundell asked.

'Insufficient evidence. Vehicles' report on the Mercedes is too open to challenge; in court, the Leston woman will probably either prevaricate or change her evidence in favour of the defence; the original identification of the crash vehicle as a Mercedes by . . . What's the name of the man?'

'Maddock.'

'Is little more than useless because the nature of his evidence would make defence counsel drool with pleasure . . . There's no attempt to understand that maybe each piece of evidence has its weaknesses, but when all are joined together they paint a picture that's clear enough even for the most short-sighted of jurors to see. The people in CPS have been so criticized in the media that now all they'll accept is a confession the archangel Gabriel will testify was voluntary.'

'So we need a hotline to Gabriel.'

'Bloody humorous!' Howes left.

It was a long time since Blundell had heard the DI swear. Why was he so uptight about this case when normally he accepted that failure was a part of life? Was it because he resented seeing someone with the Fraynes' wealth escaping the law? If so, he was being surprisingly unrealistic. Blundell quietly belched and enjoyed the slight relief that gave him; his wife had been right, he should not have had a second piece of fried bread at breakfast.

*   *   *

Lynch crossed to the right-hand display cabinet, opened
the door, reached in to alter very slightly the position of
the ornate silver snuff box which had cost him a great
deal of money because it had been claimed that it had once
belonged to Dickens, as witness the initials C.D. (After
subsequently learning that the initials almost certainly
stood for Caradoc Dewar, a noted libertine in the 1860s,
he'd arranged for the seller to spend time in hospital.)

Benson fingered the small wart that grew on the tip of
his nose. 'The facts of the case were given to the Crown
Prosecution Service to see if the Frayne woman should
be arrested and charged with running down Carol, not
reporting the accident, and leaving the scene, and the
husband charged with attempting to pervert the course
of justice by giving false information and tampering with
evidence.'

'And?'

'It's been decided that there is insufficient evidence to
make a conviction likely in either case and so it would not
be in the public interest to bring one.'

'That's the final decision?'

'No. If fresh evidence turns up, evidence which makes a
conviction much more likely, they'll have another think.'

'What are the chances of that happening?'

'Hard to say.' Benson saw Lynch's expression change.
He spoke hurriedly. 'Straight, Esme, when there's no
knowing exactly what evidence the fuzz already have,
or how much more they'll need, it's impossible to judge
the chance of them eventually fixing up a trial.'

'So?'

'What are you asking?'

'Where does that leave Carol?'

'She'll stay in the freezer until the police bring a case
or finally give up; then there's no reason for keeping her
and she'll be pushed out and buried.'

'How long before they give up?'

He shrugged his shoulders. 'It's kind of high profile with the government going on and on about driving safely and soberly. They could decide to keep the case open for months.'

'There isn't that sort of time.' Lynch crossed to one of the luxurious armchairs, sat.

'There's nothing can change things.'

Lynch joined his fingertips together and then, with a steady rhythm, separated and rejoined each pair in turn. 'I had to borrow real heavy.'

'So you've said.'

'It's costing ever heavier all the time I don't repay. And it don't do to get 'em impatient. Where's the morgue she's in?'

'On the east side of Fretstone.'

'What's the security?'

'I couldn't say.'

'Find out.'

'You ain't thinking of going in?'

'Possibly.'

'Then forget it. Don't matter what the security is, the morgue's slap alongside a copper's factory. It would be like sticking a finger in a wasps' nest.'

Lynch silently swore. Everything had been running smoothly, the wealth of Croesus had almost lain in his hands, and then that stupid cow had allowed herself to be knocked down and killed. Never trust a woman.

'Maybe something'll turn up, Esme, so as the fuzz brings a case.'

'Optimism when a moment ago it was all pessimism?' Lynch asked with heavy sarcasm.

'Anything can happen.'

'Can't you understand that I haven't time?'

Benson brought a pack of cigarettes out of his coat pocket.

'You don't smoke in this house.'

He resentfully replaced the pack.

Lynch stood and began to pace the floor. The minutes passed; he came to a stop. 'What d'you do if you come up against a locked door and haven't the key?'

'Can't say I know.'

'You get someone else to unlock it.'

'Don't forget, you'll not see me on Monday because I'm off on my holidays,' Sandra said, as she put four letters down on the desk.

'Where are you going?' Frayne asked.

'Palma Nova. I think that's in Majorca.'

'It was the last time I heard.' He picked up the first letter and began reading. 'In receive, the e comes before the i. And when a singular ends in s, the possessive adds another s.'

'Most people don't notice that sort of thing these days.'

'So you're calling me an old fuddy duddy because I do?'

She smiled.

'Since you're probably in a rush to get home, I'll make the corrections in ink and not ask you to type out the whole letter again.'

'Print. It's on the computer so I only have to make the corrections and then press the key.'

'Which I would have realized, were I not an ancient? Will you remember what the corrections are?'

'I'll try very hard to . . . What about the other letters?'

He read them. 'They're OK.'

'No split infinitives to moan about?'

'As a matter of interest, would you recognize one if you met it?'

'Of course not. I was brought up properly . . . Give me the first letter.' She took it from him. 'I'll bring it back for your signature. By the way, Mabel will be working for you while I'm away.'

'Mabel?'

'You know – older than me and wears her hair in a bun. She'll never misspell a word. And she won't ever arouse your curiosity.'

'In what way?'

'Work that out for yourself.' She chuckled, turned, and left.

Had his thoughts from time to time been obvious? If so, they didn't seem to have caused offence – perhaps on the contrary, appreciation, since they denoted a flattering interest that she knew she would not be called upon to deny. He picked up the outside phone and dialled.

'Yes?' Portia said, identifying neither herself nor the number.

'Just to let you know that I'll be back late, probably not before eight. There's a load of work which must be cleared before the weekend. Don't wait for me to have supper.'

'I'll have dinner when you return.' He should have remembered that she always ate dinner, never supper. 'Mercer was arguing again about pruning Golden Showers.'

'Presumably that's some kind of plant?'

'Don't you remember anything? It's the climbing rose I bought last autumn. If he goes on like this, we'll have to get rid of him.'

'It'll be very difficult to find someone as good.'

'I'd hardly call him good when he refuses to do as he's told.'

Perhaps that was why the garden was always in an immaculate condition.

Sixteen

'The meat is overcooked,' Portia said.
'It seems all right to me,' Frayne replied, deter-mined to be tactful.

'You said you would be back at eight, so I arranged the meal for half-past. It was after nine when you returned.'

'One piece of work took considerably longer than expected. And as a matter of fact, I did say probably not before eight rather than by eight.'

'Neither of which means after nine.'

He ate.

'Gladys has invited us to lunch on the twenty-third.'

Gladys was the widow of a minor peer; from her manner, one would have judged her late husband to have been at least an earl.

'June and Frank will also be there.'

June was a high priestess of style; in her own estimation, that was. Galliano was a close buddy; according to her, that was.

'Frank has been asked by the government to advise them on a shipping policy.'

That would ensure that the few ships remaining under the British flag would soon disappear from the seven seas.

'Are you listening to me?'

'To every word,' he assured her.

'You didn't look as though you were.'

'Ah, none but I discerned my thoughts.'

'What's that supposed to mean?'

'A very poor paraphrase.'

'Gladys once told me she frequently couldn't understand what you were talking about.'

Was that when he used words of more than one syllable?

He thought he awoke, opened his eyes, and looked up at Mickey Mouse whose face was highlighted by a torch. As in a dream, he believed both in the reality and the impossibility.

A can hissed and spray enveloped his face. He gasped for breath for a few seconds before he spiralled into unconsciousness.

A degree of comprehension returned. He realized he was lying on top of the bedclothes, his hands were tied at the wrists, his feet at the ankles. He struggled to free himself, but even though the bonds were not so tight there was no give whatsoever, it was after daybreak before he could finally pull his hands apart. He untied the cord around his feet, swivelled round on the bed, stood. He had difficulty in maintaining his balance and had to grab the corner of the bed for support; seconds later, he was violently sick.

He left the bedroom, finding it difficult to walk, and into Portia's. Her bed was empty and the bedclothes were drawn back. 'Portia!' he shouted, as he went through to the bathroom. He searched the other bedrooms and bathrooms, then the rooms downstairs. He dialled 999.

'Mickey Mouse,' Oakes said flatly. After eight years in the force, little surprised him. 'Could you see anything of the face behind the mask?'

'Nothing.'

'What about the type and colour of hair?'

'Nothing means nothing . . . What are you doing about finding my wife?' Frayne felt his stomach heave and had

135

repeatedly to swallow to prevent himself being sick for the fourth time.

'We're checking everywhere.'

'I've told you, she's not in the house or garage block.'

'I know it's very difficult for you, Mr Frayne, but in a case like this there is a routine that's best followed . . . What happened after you woke up to see the man in the mask?'

'He sprayed my face with something that knocked me out.'

'What did it smell like?'

'I was too desperately fighting for breath to worry about the smell.'

'I can imagine.' That was a white lie. Oakes seldom could imagine another's suffering, which was why he was less stressed by his work than were many others. 'Did you lose consciousness quickly?'

'It can't have taken many seconds, but it felt like hours . . . I thought I was about to die.'

'Very unpleasant,' he said, in much the same tone as he would have agreed that it was unpleasant to get one's feet wet. 'What happened when you came to?'

'I was bloody sick . . .' About to say more, Frayne came to a sharp stop because the words threatened to promote his stomach into yet more feverish activity.

A PC stepped into the room. 'All checked outside, Ken.'

'Have you found my wife?' Frayne demanded.

'I'm afraid there's no sign of her.'

'She's got to be somewhere.'

'She's not in the house, the outbuildings, or the garden,' the PC said stolidly.

'You've got to find her.'

'We're doing everything we can, Mr Frayne,' Oakes said. 'Now, when you came to, was there any sound suggesting someone was still in the house?'

136

'God Almighty! What does all this matter if they've got her? Why aren't you searching for her?'

'Until we can establish all the facts, we've nothing to suggest where to start looking.'

The PC said: 'How many cars do you run, Mr Frayne?'

He forced himself to be calmer. 'An Audi and a Mercedes.'

'Are both here?' Oakes asked.

The PC nodded.

'Did you check the boots?'

'Empty.'

'Get on the blower and tell 'em that it's confirmed Mrs Frayne is missing.'

'I told you that,' Frayne said furiously, calm forgotten. 'You've wasted all this time.'

'We've been making certain, as we had to,' Oakes said as the PC left the room. 'Do you know of anyone who might wish to harm Mrs Frayne?'

'Of course I don't.'

'Have you received any threats in the recent past?'

'No.'

'And your wife hasn't mentioned receiving any?'

'No.'

'Has anything been stolen?'

'You think I've bothered to find that out when I know she's missing?'

'We'd better do so now.'

'And waste more time?'

'Mr Frayne, if things have been stolen, we're probably looking for straight thieves – that's important to know.'

'If they're thieves, why would they take my wife?'

'It's not possible to say right now . . . We'll go round the house and you can tell me if anything's missing. Is there a safe?'

'Yes.'

'We'll start with that. Will you show me where it is?'

The safe was locked.

Ten minutes later, they were in the dining room. 'Some silver's missing,' Frayne said.

'What silver would that be?'

'There were three pieces there.' He pointed at the sideboard.

'What are they like?'

'Two helmet-shaped ewers by Paul de Lamerie and a Carolean sugar bowl.'

'Are they valuable?'

'Yes. The sugar bowl especially.'

'Do you have photographs of them and are they insured?'

'Yes.'

'Later on, let me have the photographs so as we can have them copied; and I'll need the insurance valuation.'

'Could my wife have heard the intruders, come downstairs and found them taking the silver, and they . . .' He became silent.

'There's no way of judging. Best not to start imagining.'

'How do I stop myself doing that?'

Oakes didn't try to answer. 'We'll finish down here, then go back upstairs and look around the other rooms to see if anything's missing there.'

One part of Frayne's mind could accept that this methodical response had to be the correct one, another part silently shouted at them to do something far more direct to find Portia.

Howes yawned twice. 'I'm too old to be dragged out early in the morning.'

Aren't we all? Blundell thought.

Howes picked up the styrofoam cup and drank. 'It's worse than when the canteen made the coffee.'

'It is hot and wet.'

'So's bath water . . . What are we looking at?'

'On the face of things, a straightforward burglary that probably turned sour. One, more likely two, men went into her bedroom to knock her out, as they had her husband, but either she was awake or was woken and tried to reach for the panic alarm button. There was a struggle, she ripped off the mask of one of 'em and since she could now identify this chummy they had to make certain she wouldn't. So they took her off with them.'

'Why not kill her then and there?'

'Perhaps they saw an opportunity for ransom.'

'When they're taking her off because she can visually identify one of 'em?'

'If no money's paid, they cut her throat; if money is paid, they collect and then cut her throat.'

'Do you see that as the most likely scenario?'

'No.'

Howes began to tap on the desk with his fingers. 'We've not been receiving any whispers of a thieving mob hard enough to murder. But maybe this lot got together just for the one job . . . You said something about facts which don't seem to add up?'

'The outer doors of Bell's House have good, real solid locks, yet the intruders found no problem in forcing the two on the scullery door. Oates asked the SOCO to check the internals of those two locks and he says they're almost clear.'

'What exactly does he mean by that?'

'One or two very faint marks. These could have been caused by the keys having slight play or they could mark the work of a twirler who's so good he's next door to genius. How many of them are there in the world? And one of them would want heavy money to work. Who's going to offer that sort of dosh to crack an ordinary home?'

'Is that all?'

'Just the beginning. There's a good alarm system and Mr Frayne swears it was set by him before he went to

bed. Yet it never tripped and there's no sign of inter-
ference.'

'The villains are beginning to sound real smart.'

'Yet they overlooked the safe which normally would be
the first thing they'd check. Oates got Mr Frayne to open
it up. He says he's never seen such an array of jewellery
outside the Tower of London. There was enough to keep
a dozen villains on the Costa del Crime for the rest of
their lives.'

'They might have found the safe was too solid for
them.'

'A mob with a twirler as good as those door locks name
him, and an electronics expert capable of bypassing an
alarm system without trace, would have a household safe
open in between puffs of a cigarette.

'And there's one last thing. Mr Frayne told Oates that
when he came to his wrists were tied in front of him. The
cord was tight, but not as tight as it could have been, so after
a long struggle he was able to free himself. Whoever tied
him up didn't know to secure the elbows together behind
the back because then the victim's going to starve to death
before he gets free. A smart chummy learns that with his
mother's milk.'

'You're calling this a faked break-in?'

'I'm saying it could easily be.'

Howes finally ceased tapping his fingers. 'The Fraynes
know we've identified her as the driver of the car which
killed Carol Fowler, but they can't be certain how close
we are to arresting 'em. Scared people always think the
worst. They reckon we're about to jump. He works out
an unoriginal way of saving her – fake a break-in and an
abduction. That leaves her free to take off to where?'

'Anywhere the rich feel safe.'

'It makes sense.'

'So we . . .'

'Don't openly act on that assumption as yet.'

'Why not?'

'Because we don't have hard proof, which means we could be made to appear to be hopelessly wrong and then, since they've got real financial clout, we could watch our pensions float away. We play it softly, softly. That means as quietly as possible finding out whether she's been selling shares, moving money out of the country, all the things one does if one wants to lead a comfortable, anonymous life abroad.'

Seventeen

Frayne found himself questioning whether he should be eating breakfast when Portia was missing, perhaps being subjected to . . . Stress scrambled a person's brains. Whether or not he ate could not alter facts . . .

Yet again, he tried to make sense of what had happened, yet again, his imagination pictured her in the hands of men who believed compassion to be a weakness. Why hadn't they just knocked her out with the spray, tied her up, and left her? He'd asked the police that several times and not one of them had answered. Because their experience suggested the worst?

He drank a second cup of coffee. The police had been so damn methodical. Logic had agreed they had every reason to be, emotion had shouted at them for their slow approach in a situation where every minute must be critical. Yet what was the nature of that emotion? Love? It would be hypocritical to claim that it was his passionate love for her which fuelled his panicky fears. Theirs had become a marriage only in name. Yet he would never have wished her harm, not even when she had used her financial power to make him betray himself . . .

The front doorbell rang. He waited for Enid to find out who the caller was. The bell rang a second time. He remembered it was a Saturday so Enid had not, as he should have realized, come that morning . . .

He went through to the hall, opened the front door.

'Morning, Mr Frayne,' Roach said.

'Have you found her?'

'I'm afraid there's no news.'

'Then why aren't you looking for her?'

'There are some things you can tell us that could well help us find her so it's more important right now for me to listen than to act.'

'I . . . I'm sorry. I'm being illogical.'

'With every reason.'

'Come on in.'

Roach entered. Frayne shut the door. 'What is it you want to know?'

'It may take a little time so would it be a good idea to sit?'

'Yes, of course. I'm . . .' Absurdly, he found himself hesitant to say he had been eating because that might give the impression of heartlessness – even though he had only moments ago assured himself it did not. He said, in a rush of words: 'I'm just finishing breakfast. Would you like something to eat or drink?'

'Nothing to eat, thanks, but a cup of coffee would be great.'

Frayne led the way into the morning room, said he'd make the coffee. In the kitchen, he refilled the machine, put this on the stove.

He returned, sat. 'Coffee's making; it won't be long.'

'Sorry to cause trouble.'

'It's no trouble.' They must sound like a stilted social meeting, he suddenly thought irrationally. 'What is it you want to know?' he asked for the second time.

'It's like this, Mr Frayne. To be frank, at this moment we have no idea where Mrs Frayne is, or why she was kidnapped. So until we have a definite lead, we can only go along eliminating certain possibilities. Let's start by asking you about Mrs Frayne's handbag. Ken – the DC you spoke to last night – says you couldn't find it. Have you had another look for it?'

'No.'

'Perhaps you'd do that in a minute.'

'I'll do it now.'

'Why not finish . . .'

He ignored the other and left. Portia's handbag would be up in her bedroom, on a small shelf in the kitchen (never left there when Enid would be in the house; staff could not be trusted), or in the blue room.

It was not in her bedroom or the blue room. He returned to the kitchen. It was not there and the machine had completed its cycle. He poured coffee into one jug, milk into another, brought sugar bowl from one cupboard and cup and saucer from a second one – not the formal, affected setting it would have been if he had been preparing everything for Portia . . .

He carried the tray through to the morning room. 'I can't find the handbag.' He sat. He poured coffee into the cup, passed that across, indicated the milk and sugar, topped up his own cup.

'Does Mrs Frayne usually carry a large amount of cash in her handbag?' Roach asked.

'Probably never more than fifty pounds.'

'Does she have credit or debit cards?'

'Four or five.'

'Do you have a list of the numbers and whether they're Mastercard, American Express, or whatever? Or maybe they're listed on a card-protection scheme, in which case I'll get on to them for details and ask them to make certain we're informed if any attempt is made to use a card.'

'You think that's likely?'

'It's possible. Likewise, I need to know what bank accounts your wife has. And it will help us a lot if you'll give your written permission for us to ask the bank for details of any movements in her accounts.' Past as well as present, Roach thought.

'What do you really think has happened?' Frayne asked.

'I was being totally honest when I told you that unfortunately we just don't know yet.'

'Could she have been kidnapped for ransom money?'

'That has to be one of the possibilities. Of course, if you receive any sort of demand, you'll get in touch with us immediately, won't you, no matter what threats are made to try to prevent you doing that?'

Frayne nodded. He fiddled with the handle of his cup. 'My wife is inclined to be rather . . . To have them seeing her in a nightdress . . .' He stopped.

'Best not to think about it.'

'That's been said before. And when I asked, "How do I stop myself?" there wasn't any answer.'

'It's so much easier to give advice than to act on it . . . Did Ken ask you last night if any of your wife's clothing was missing?'

'I can't remember.'

'Then you haven't checked?'

'No. And in any case, I doubt I could tell since she has so many clothes.'

'Nevertheless, perhaps you'll have a go at it?'

'Surely to God they aren't likely to have stolen her frocks?'

'It happens, Mr Frayne; there's not much that doesn't happen.' As he finished speaking, Roach realized that in the circumstances, his words had been ill chosen. But they could not be unspoken. 'There's one thing more. I'd like to see her passport.'

'Why?'

'Passports are worth surprisingly good money these days, so if hers has been stolen, we'll circulate the details and should anyone try to make use of it by changing the photo, and so on, that person can be identified. Would you know where it's likely to be?'

'In the safe.'

'Then later on, perhaps you'd get it for me.'

145

A quarter of an hour later, in the library, Frayne swung back the small section of false books – an unconvincing camouflage – to reveal the safe, dialled the combination, and opened it. A quick search failed to uncover her passport although it was usually with his on the bottom shelf; a longer and far more thorough check of all the contents had the same negative result.

'Was she planning to go abroad?' Roach asked.

'There's been no mention of the idea.'

'Give us a ring if you come across it, will you? . . . That about covers everything, so I'll get out of your way as quickly as I can.'

Roach put the several sheets of paper down on Blundell's desk. 'A list of credit and debit cards obtained from the card-protection scheme – they've been alerted – and her bank accounts; also husband's permission to talk to the banks. He can't find her handbag and says she's so many clothes, he simply can't judge if any are missing.'

Blundell skimmed through what was written. 'She's more bank accounts than a dog has fleas.'

'When you're that rich, I suppose you have to spread things around to keep ahead of the tax man.'

'What's the number of her mobile, if she has one, and which company handles her calls?'

'Sorry, I forgot to find out.'

'D'you think you can strain your brain and remember to get back on to him and find out, then check if there have been any calls in the past twenty-four hours . . . No doubt you also forgot to ask him about her passport.'

'It's usually held in the safe. He looked and said it wasn't there.'

'Surprise! Surprise!'

'It could have been taken, Sarge.'

'Having nicked the silver, they open up the safe and inside is a fortune in jewellery and a passport. So being real intelligent, they take the passport?' As always, Blundell's sarcasm was crude.

'There could be a reason why they just took just that.'

'There could be a reason why pigs don't have wings, only it's difficult to think what that could be since they aren't birds.'

'I've a feeling there's an odd slant to this case.'

'Try keeping your head upright.'

'Mr Frayne said something which made me think. He's really worried because his wife was in a nightdress and since she's prudish, that would have made everything so much more appalling for her . . . If he's so concerned over something like that, it makes it seem she really has been abducted.'

'My son, the hay seeds are thick about your collar. He has to try to convince us she's been kidnapped and not taken off on a cruise to the West Indies. What, he asks himself, is the best way of doing that? Easily done if it's DC Roach asks the questions. Just tell him things which he thinks only an innocent man might say.'

'Go along that road and you'll end up not believing a word.'

'At last, a glimmer of intelligence!'

Eighteen

On Sundays diving was allowed in the larger of the two lakes, Steelwater, provided there was proper supervision by a qualified supervisor. Thirty yards back from the water on the western side there was a small wooden hut in which equipment could be stored during the day – permanent storage was inadvisable because of the risk of vandalism and theft – and in inclement weather onlookers could shelter as they watched – as exciting an occupation, a long-suffering wife had remarked, as watching paint dry.

After a brief reminder of all they had been told and a careful check of equipment, Williams led the three beginners down to the water. When knee deep, he called a halt and again reminded them to keep in visual contact at all times. He did not miss the sneering impatience of the twenty-year-old redhead; cocky little sod, he thought. It was his kind who could almost be guaranteed to cause trouble.

Face masks and breathing tubes were fitted and thumbs were raised to show all was well. Williams motioned them forward. The only woman – a trim figure, but unfortunate looks due to protruding teeth – was on his right. The redhead, who'd already forged ahead of the line – wanting to show how strong and active he was? – came to a sudden stop. He moved to his right, then dropped down beneath the surface. Alarmed – an undeclared epileptic, now having a fit? – Williams surged forward as quickly as the chest-deep water allowed. The redhead stood up so suddenly they almost collided. Williams swore, then removed his mask and tube. 'What's the problem?' he asked, as pleasantly as he could bring himself to be – their fees provided his, untaxed, weekend income.

'I kicked something,' the redhead replied. 'Can't make it out, but it's quite a size.'

'Things get chucked here. Best see what it is in case it can be a danger.' He fitted mask and tube, dropped beneath the surface. There was considerable silt and this had become disturbed, reducing visibility. He reached out and touched a bundle which, as he passed his hands along it, he determined had been lashed with cord. He surfaced. 'We'd best get it ashore.'

'What d'you reckon it is?'

'Could be anything. Give us a hand.'

The cord made it relatively easy to gain a grip, but despite the buoyancy provided by the water, the bundle was heavy; when it needed to be lifted out of the water, Williams called across the other man to help them. They lifted it out and carried it a few feet up on to the shallow, grassy bank. The covering was a blanket with three bars of colour running along it.

'It smells a bit,' said the woman. 'What on earth can it be?'

'Easiest thing to do is find out,' said the redhead. He pulled at an edge of the blanket and after a struggle managed to draw this back until he could see what was inside. 'Jesus!' he exclaimed, his voice high.

'What is it?' She moved forward and then for several seconds made a whimpering sound at the back of her throat as she stared at the hand, the skin of which was markedly wrinkled; then she stumbled away and was sick.

Police tape laid out in a semicircle had sealed off a considerable area and beyond this, drawn by an interest none would have wished to try to explain, were several onlookers. Within the semicircle a large plastic sheet had been laid out on the ground and the bundle carefully placed in the centre of this. The detective inspector and detective sergeant stood on one side, occasionally talking to each other, but mostly silent. Two scene-of-crime officers, having photographed and videoed the bundle both before it had been moved and after it had been placed on the plastic sheet, morosely wondered why it always seemed to be a Sunday when they were called out. Two PCs stood around, ready to carry out crowd control should this be needed.

The arrival of a grey Saab sharpened the scene. The DI and the DS walked up the very shallow slope to the car, one of the SOCOs checked how much unused tape remained in the camcorder and the two PCs began to pace their beat. The pathologist, tall, thin, with aquiline features, and a moustache of which only he approved, climbed out of the car. 'Good morning.'

'Good morning, sir,' the DI replied. 'Traffic's very bad this morning, then?'

'No worse than usual,' the pathologist replied, ignoring the inference that his dilatoriness had kept everyone waiting. He went round to the boot, lifted the lid, brought out surgical overalls. 'What exactly have we got?'

'Four people were making their first dives when one of 'em struck something with his foot. The instructor checked, found it was a bundle and decided to bring it ashore. Someone was curious to find out what was inside and saw a hand.'

'As good a cure as any for curiosity.'

The remark annoyed the DI.

'Male, female, or modern androgynous question mark?'

'From the size and weight, an adult body, and from the rings on the finger, female.'

'Let's get started; I've a luncheon invitation I've been ordered not to miss . . . You can bring my gear.'

The DI nodded at the DS. Just a bloody porter, the detective sergeant thought as he went round the car to the boot. He lifted out a suitcase with sides that were reinforced with brass fittings.

Every knot was photographed before it was undone; the unrolling of the sodden blanket was videoed; the body, tied into a foetal position by similar cord to that which had been used for the outer lashings, was videoed and photographed from several angles – that done, the lace-edged nightdress was pulled down to hide her sex in a gesture that brought a touch of humanity to the scene; very close-up photos were taken of the cord which was wound round her neck and pulled so tight that in one place the flesh had overlapped it; photos were taken of the slab of concrete which had been used as ballast.

The pathologist finished his examination and stripped off the surgical gloves he had been wearing. 'There's almost no doubt she was strangled with that cord – the usual Tardieu spots are in evidence. Rigor's passing, but not completely gone, which suggests death was between two and four days ago, but that's an even rougher guide than usual; water complicates everything. I may be able to tell you more after the PM, but don't bank on that.' He began to walk briskly towards his car. 'Wealthy background.'

'Why exactly d'you say that?' asked the DI, who was having to walk very briskly because his legs were considerably shorter than the other's.

'I know a little about jewellery – no expert, of course – and those rings suggest heavy money. Another thing, the nightdress is very good quality silk and the lacework is of the highest quality; my wife couldn't begin to afford that sort of gear.'

He climbed into the Saab and drove off. The DI phoned county HQ and asked for a divers' team to be sent to the lake to make a search around the area where the body had been found. He then supervised the bagging and logging of all the evidence and the removal of the body.

Nineteen

B lundell looked into the DI's room, found it empty, continued on to the CID general room. Lipman was working at one of the desks. 'Have you seen the Guv'nor, Reg?'

'Not so far this morning.'

'Then he isn't coming in.'

'Some are lucky. Is there a problem?'

'That's for him to decide.' He walked over to the desk on which the outside phone, which had a very long lead, had been left. He lifted the receiver, dialled. 'Morning, Mrs Howes, it's Sergeant Blundell . . . Yes, I do realize it's a Sunday and the Guv'nor needs time off, but an important matter has just surfaced . . . I'm afraid he will have to deal with it, yes . . . No, I wouldn't if it weren't really necessary . . . Thank you.'

'A bollocking from the missus?' Lipman asked cheerfully.

The minutes passed. Then Blundell said: 'Sorry to trouble you just before the Sunday roast, sir . . . I'm very afraid it does . . . We've just received word from A division that a woman's body, wrapped in a blanket, has been pulled out of Steelwater Lake. They got in touch with us because the description matches the one of Mrs Frayne we've circulated . . . Just a nightdress . . . No distinguishing marks, but there are two rings on her fingers apart from a wedding one . . . No, we don't know that . . . I can't

153

really say, sir . . . Yes, I do . . . I'll find out right away.'
He replaced the receiver.

'Something tells me you're not his flavour of the month!'
Lipman said.

'Something tells me you need to learn a sight more
respect for your seniors. But right now, you're to drive
out to Frayne's place.'

'She's not in the Bahamas enjoying a life of luxury
after all?'

'Looks that way. Ask him what rings his wife would
have been wearing and can he describe her night clothes.
If the answers are a fancy silk nightdress with yards of lace
and in addition to the wedding ring, a solitaire diamond and
a square ruby surrounded by diamonds, warn him a body
has been recovered and we've reason to think it may be
his wife's and he'll be called on to identify her.'

'That'll just make his Sunday.'

'If he starts shedding tears, you'll know he's got big
teeth and bad breath.'

'How's that?'

'Crocodile tears.'

'I still don't get it.'

'Don't they teach you even that much these days?'

Frayne crossed the hall and opened the front door. The
caller reminded him of the maths master who had tried,
and failed, to interest him in calculus.

'Detective Constable Lipman, local CID, Mr Frayne.'

'You've heard something?'

'That's right.'

'What?'

'Maybe I could come in?'

Frayne held the door wide open for Lipman to enter.
'What's happened?' he asked, as he closed the door.

'Before I answer that, perhaps you'll tell me what Mrs
Frayne was wearing Friday night when she was in bed?'

Frayne stared at him for several seconds, then looked away. 'Why are you asking that?'

'I'll explain in a minute.'

After a while, he said: 'Naturally, she was wearing night clothes.'

'Which would be what?'

'A nightdress.'

'Can you describe it?'

'Not the particular one she had on that night, no.'

'You didn't see her in bed?'

'We sleep in separate rooms,' Frayne said curtly.

He should have remembered the other claimed to have been in a different bedroom from his wife when he was surprised by Mickey Mouse. 'Can you suggest what it was most likely to have been like?'

'Silk, probably white or cream.'

'Would there have been some trimmings?'

'Considerable lacework.'

'What jewellery would she have been wearing?'

'I think her pearls have been sent for restringing, so it would have been her engagement ring and possibly one or two others.'

'What does her engagement ring look like?'

'A fairly large solitaire diamond.' Which she had bought and then proudly shown to everyone, claiming it was a family heirloom which her great-grandmother had worn.

'And the other rings?'

'She has several.'

'Does she have a ruby ring?'

'Two.'

'Would one have been a square ruby surrounded by diamonds?'

'Yes.'

The questions should have warned him what was to come, Lipman thought, but a guilty man often seemed relatively dull-witted, perhaps unable to comprehend that his crime was about to become unravelled. 'I am sorry to have to tell you, but earlier this morning, the body of a female was brought out of Steelwater Lake. She was wearing a white silk nightdress with a lot of lace and on her fingers, in addition to a gold wedding ring, two other rings which seem to match the descriptions you've mentioned.'

'You . . . you're saying my wife is dead?'

'There can be no certainty until a definite identification, which is why you'll be asked to make this.'

'When?'

'I can't say except it will be soon. We'll be in touch and . . .'

'Perhaps you'll leave.'

Lipman hesitated, then turned, opened the door and went out.

Frayne stared into black-edged space. There was no certainty yet, yet there was clearly certainty. Mickey Mouse had murdered her. Why? In God's name, why? He accepted he was not suffering the overwhelming grief of lost love, but his bewilderment seemed almost as bitter. For him, there had been very little time between being awoken by the masked man and losing consciousness, but terror had stretched seconds into hours; how much worse had it been for her? Had they killed her immediately, had they forced her to leave with them and killed her outside, had they waited to kill her until . . . ? A man's mind could crucify him. He had to find a way of stilling his, however temporarily.

Twenty minutes later, he passed through Larnhurst, bore right and then almost immediately left, and turned into the driveway of Thoburn Cottage.

As he approached the outer front door, Francesca opened it. 'I'm sorry, Dick,' she said briskly, 'but I'm just off to see Bill—' She stopped abruptly. 'You look as if something awful has happened,' she finally said, far from briskly.

'It has.'

'Then you'd better come on in.'

'But if you're on your way to . . .'

'If I can somehow help you, that'll be doing more good than sitting in a lounge with half a dozen zombies and making conversation to someone who's in another world while I'm wondering how soon my conscience will let me escape.'

He entered and followed her into the sitting room. She sat on the settee. 'What's gone wrong?'

He told her.

'I'm so very sorry,' she said. 'I wish there were something I could do to help.'

'Don't you understand that just sitting here helps me?' Some women had an almost infinite capacity for offering sympathy, much of it wordless.

On Monday morning, Roach stepped out of the building into the car park, saw Blundell was about to drive out in the CID Rover, held up his hand to stop the other, hurried across.

'What the hell is it?' Blundell demanded through the lowered window.

'There's a message just in from county HQ. The diving team that has been searching Steelwater Lake have come up with a sack in which are three pieces of silver.'

'Should have been twenty . . . Two something or other and one something else?'

'That sounds about right.'

'One more nail in Frayne's coffin.'

'I don't quite see that.'

'You can't appreciate that if you're told someone broke into a house to steal whatever was going and later what was stolen is found chucked into a lake, something smells?'

'On the face of things, yes. But I keep remembering how

157

I got the impression that Mr Frayne was dead scared his wife would be sexually assaulted.'

'Forget your impressions and remember there were hardly any marks in the outside door locks, that this smart twirler busted the safe and took the passport but not the jewellery, that a mob so cool could not tie Frayne up so as he would be secure, that she was throttled and thrown into the lake without having her valuable rings removed.'

'The very fact that so many things don't add up . . .'

'Well?'

'It just seems things don't make sense.'

'I'm on my way to take Frayne to the morgue. Now if he says it's not his missus, then that will be something that doesn't make any bloody sense . . . Stand clear if you don't want to have knocked out of you the few senses you may still have.' Blundell drove off.

It was not the devastatingly sickening experience Frayne had feared. The signs marking the beginning of putrefaction had been camouflaged, the facial skin had been eased and teased until Portia's expression had become puzzlement rather than agony.

'Can you identify her?' Blundell asked quietly, not in deference to Frayne's feelings, but because in his opinion the morgue, as did a church, demanded at least the appearance of respectful reverence.

'My wife,' Frayne answered bleakly.

Blundell nodded. The attendant brought the sheet up and over her face, then waited for them to leave before he slid her back into the refrigerated unit.

Benson waited to speak until Ferdinand, clearly piqued at having been ordered out of the room, had left and closed the door behind himself. 'My information is that Frayne has been asked to identify his wife's body.'

Lynch leaned back in the chair, which creaked, despite

having cost him just over a thousand pounds. 'So that's the end of trying to prove who knocked Carol over?'

'It does seem most unlikely the police will charge the husband with an attempt to pervert the course of justice when the principal is dead and he's almost certain to be charged with her murder.'

'So will they be releasing Carol's body right away?'

'It's difficult . . .'

'Don't goddamn well start telling me it's difficult to say.'

'But things aren't quite so simple as you think.'

'If the police reckon it was the Frayne woman who ran Carol down and now there's no way of charging her, where's the difficulty?'

'They still may not release Carol's body for burial in the foreseeable future.'

'Why the hell not?'

'You made it seem the husband did the murder.'

'Of course I did. If there wasn't an obvious motive for the killing, the police might have started thinking for once.'

'Sure, but if the husband's the only suspect, the police may see Carol as an important part of his motive.'

'What are you on about now?'

'Don't you see, Esme, they'll need a motive for the murder. Money, sure. But he's been living with her for several years and quite happily spending her money so why should he suddenly want to change things when to do so is bound to be bloody risky? The police are likely going to say to themselves, maybe the death of Carol was a lot more complicated than we reckoned at the time. Whilst that thought's around, they could maybe not release Carol's body.'

Lynch swore.

'Maybe after a bit . . .'

'Don't you understand a sodding thing? I can't wait, I borrowed heavy.'

'I know . . .'

'It's costing me heavy every extra day.'

'Yes, but . . .'

'Find out how good the security of the morgue is.'

'I told you, it's next door to the cop shop . . .'

'A sharp team will laugh.'

'A team that sharp is really going to cost.'

'And they'll get paid when I have the body.'

'They'll want it up front.'

'D'you think I've got that sort of bread when I'm having to try to keep the others happy?'

'You'll have to find it if you really want a break-in at the morgue.'

Lynch, his expression suggesting pain, turned his head and looked at the nearer display cabinet and the snuff boxes in it.

Howes sat at the round table in the conference room and wondered why Newby had not retired when rumour had promised he would. Theirs was not a happy relationship. The detective chief superintendent made no secret of his contempt for arse-polishers – the term he used to describe officers who were content to sit and let events direct them rather than directing events.

'Have you checked out the husband's finances?' Newby asked.

'Not yet, sir,' Howes replied. 'But that's in hand.'

'Shorthand for saying it's not been started.'

'It's a question of priorities . . .'

'The solution of which obviously escapes you.'

The DCS's wife had recently divorced him after twenty-five years of marriage. The first look at his close-set eyes, beaky nose, thin mouth, and square jaw, could and should have warned her.

'Mrs Frayne's wealthy, isn't she?'

'By most people's standards, I'd guess she's very wealthy.'

'Yet you haven't even started to find out if he's been hanging on to her financial coat-tails.'

Howes inwardly sighed. 'I reckon we can be certain he's not in her league. He has a job with Andrew and Sachs, a local firm, and according to reputation, they're not generous with their salaries. He may have some capital, of course, but . . .'

'How does he figure in her will?'

'I can't say yet.'

'Something more that's just in hand?'

There was brief silence.

'You're certain she was driving the car that killed the Fowler woman?'

'Yes.'

'But never got around to charging her.'

'The CPS reckoned there wasn't enough evidence to warrant her arrest.'

'So what stopped you turning up more?'

'Her husband was supporting her story, which was just sharp enough when Winifred Leston, a friend, half-heartedly backed her alibi.'

'If it was half-hearted, it wasn't the truth. Why didn't you pressure Leston to find out what that was?'

'In my judgement, sir, not a woman to respond to pressure.'

'Because you can't work out what form it should take? Is there a connection between Mrs Frayne's killing Carol Fowler and being murdered? If she had lived and eventually been convicted with the help of fresh evidence, the husband would have been facing a serious charge.'

'I have considered that.'

'And?'

'It seems rather a light motive.'

'Haven't you ever seen lighter?'

'Yes, sir,' Howes replied reluctantly.

'Is there a third party with a motive for the murder?'

'There's no suggestion of anyone so far.'

'Was it a happy marriage?'

'I doubt it. She was all ice.'

'Let a woman hold the purse strings and she becomes a second Adolf.'

Howes enjoyed the pleasant possibility that Newby's venom was because his ex-wife had had more money than he.

'Has Frayne got a girlfriend?'

'There's hardly been the time to find out . . .'

'Time is something a good detective makes. What staff is there?'

'At Bell's House? There's a daily, but I can't say what hours she works, and there's a gardener – from the size and look of the garden, he's probably full-time.'

'They'll be able to tell us a lot more than you can. Have comparison blanket and cord gone along to the forensic lab?'

'Not yet.'

'Why not?'

'When you informed me you were taking direct charge of the case, sir, I assumed all major decisions should be yours because the moment Frayne learns what we're doing, he'll understand he's a possible suspect.'

'Unless he's a moron, he'll realize that now. The husband's always a suspect, especially when he comes up with a story of being woken up by Mickey Mouse. What self-respecting villain is going to walk around looking like a bloody mouse?'

'More likely to be Roland.'

'What's that?'

'Roland Rat. D'you remember the old television series for kids . . .'

'No.'

Why, Howes wondered morosely, did his attempts at humour so often fail?

'I want comparison materials sent to the lab. I want to know the contents of her will; what his financial status is; any history of domestic rows; what girlfriends he has and whether he's been talking about taking 'em on round-the-world cruises. And get things moving now, not have 'em in hand in a fortnight's time.'

'It's very early days,' said the elderly solicitor. 'Probate hasn't been applied for, let alone granted, it will undoubtedly be quite a time before letters of administration—'

'All we're asking for,' Oakes said, interrupting what threatened to be a dissertation on the laws of inheritance, 'is the identity of the main beneficiary. The will will eventually be made public, won't it?'

'Of course. But regard has to be given to the word "eventually".'

'Look, sir, let's put it like this. Is the lucky one the husband? Maybe you'd rather not name names, so what say I suggest it is him and you don't correct me unless I'm wrong?'

The elderly solicitor took off his glasses and polished them with a handkerchief.

'Thanks,' Oakes said.

'I wish you to understand that I have been considering your request, not responding to it.'

Lawyers covered themselves with shields, not glory, Oakes thought as he left.

Twenty

Enid opened the front door. 'Good morning,' Blundell said. 'We'd like a word with Mr Frayne.'

'He ain't in,' she answered as, for no good reason, she looked disapprovingly at Roach.

'Have you any idea when he'll be back?'

'Can't say.'

'Then perhaps we can have a word with you?'

'What about?'

'One or two things that have to be discussed following the tragic death of Mrs Frayne. You must find that very sad.'

'Must I?'

Her response confused Blundell, who was always careful to observe convention whatever his private feelings.

'Shall we come in?' Roach said, moving forward as he spoke.

She automatically stepped aside so they could enter, then was annoyed she had done so. 'I ain't got nothing to say,' she snapped.

'I'm sure you can help us,' Blundell said pleasantly.

She hesitated, finally led the way across the hall to one of the five doorways where she came to a halt, her hand on the door handle. 'We'd best go in here because I ain't finished the other rooms. Are your shoes clean?'

'What's that?' Blundell asked, once more confused.

'She don't like dirty shoes on her carpets what is so valuable. Or so she says.'

'We could walk across fresh fallen snow without dirtying a single flake,' Roach assured her.

She sniffed loudly as she opened the door of the green room.

As he sat on one of the luxuriously upholstered chairs, Blundell carefully kept his shoes on the parquet floor and well clear of the very large Caucasian dragon carpet which filled the room with colour.

'What is it, then?' she asked. 'I've too much work to do to waste me time.'

'So we'll be as quick as we can,' Blundell assured her. 'I'd like you to think if you know of anyone who might have hated Mrs Frayne so much that they'd do this dreadful thing? Of course, it's not nice naming someone, but we can promise that what you say won't go beyond these four walls and it could really help us . . .'

It was some time before he asked her a specifically relevant question. His mode of questioning would have aroused the contempt of the detective chief superintendent, who believed in always being forceful. But there were witnesses, and Enid was one, who would provide him with information that Newby would fail to elicit.

'Nothing was ever right,' she said, in answer to what he had asked her. 'Like when she swore it was just dust under the bureau after I told her it was woodworm . . .' It was a short story made long.

'It sounds as if she could be very difficult?'

'That she could!' There were occasions when Enid was far from taciturn. 'She found one of her dresses was torn and said I'd done that. I told her, I don't never touch her stuff unless she leaves it around and then it's her fault . . .' It was a convoluted story, the logic of which became lost.

'And is Mr Frayne as difficult as she was?'

'Can't say that,' she answered quickly. 'He'll have a chat and a bit of a laugh, which she wouldn't.'

'But they got on well together, despite being rather different?'

'Most of the time, I suppose.'

'Not always?'

'Didn't often see 'em together, him being at work during the week and me not usually here at weekends. But I've been here when there's times . . .' She stopped.

'Things weren't so calm?'

'What d'you expect? I've heard her going on at him because she had to buy this house, not him, and pay for running it; and come to that, most anything else she could think to moan about. If I was to speak to my Bert like she did to him, he'd complain, no mistake!'

'How did Mr Frayne react to that sort of thing?'

'Most times, he'd just laugh or say something a bit silly.'

'But not always?'

'He's a sharp tongue when he wants. And she didn't like it when he used it.'

'She'd go for him even more?'

'That she would.'

'All in all, it doesn't sound like it was the happiest of marriages.'

'It weren't.'

'I suppose that's why she saw quite a bit of her friend,' Roach said, to Blundell's surprise.

She turned to face Roach. 'What friend?'

'Miss Leston.'

'Her!'

'You know her?'

'She's been here often enough. Mostly when he's been at work, of course.'

'Why d'you say that?'

'Why d'you think?'

Blundell's expression suggested he was having difficulty in accepting the suggestion of a relationship which until then he had considered ridiculous.

Roach said. 'Does Mr Frayne like Miss Leston?'

'He wouldn't be much of a man to do that, would he?'

'Did he ever complain to his wife about her friendship with Miss Leston?'

'Never heard him do so.'

Until something had to be accepted, it could be ignored. 'I suppose if she had her friend, like as not, he had his?'

There was a silence.

'Does he have one?' Blundell asked quietly.

She fingered her upper lip.

'He'll never hear from us what you say.'

'Well . . .'

'Yes?'

'Can't be certain. It's just . . . Mrs Frayne had just gone out when he was back early in the afternoon and didn't know I was here – couldn't come in the morning – and I heard him talking on the phone.'

'To a woman?'

'Ever heard of a man called Francesca?'

'So what was he saying?'

'Talking about someone called Bill – sounded like her husband – what was in a home because his mind was gone; he was saying she musn't blame herself on account of there being no way she could keep him in the house when he couldn't look after himself and kept falling and she couldn't lift him, not without help.'

'Was he speaking affectionately?'

'Wouldn't say so, not especially, that is.'

'Then what makes you think Francesca is a special kind of a friend?'

'Didn't say I did.'

'True enough, you didn't. Only it did seem that was what you were suggesting.'

'I wasn't suggesting nothing.' She paused. 'It's only that when he comes out of the room and sees me . . . Well, you can always tell when a man's been up to something.'

167

'How?' Roach asked curiously.

'Because he's like he's been caught with his trousers down.'

Roach laughed.

'I reckon you know what I mean, right enough,' she said belligerently.

Blundell said: 'You think that seeing you and knowing you could have overheard him gave him a guilty conscience?'

'All I'm saying is what he looked like when he saw me.'

'Do you know which of their friends is called Francesca?'

'No.'

'He didn't mention any other name over the phone?'

'No.'

'Maybe she's just a friend they haven't seen recently.'

She muttered bad-temperedly, annoyed because it seemed they were not accepting her seriously.

'There is just one more thing. Are there any double-size blankets in the house which are the colour of straw and have three bands of different colours across the top?'

'Suppose there is?'

'You can tell me what the three colours are.'

'Why d'you want to know?'

'It could be important.'

After a moment, she said: 'There's some with two red stripes and one blue in between . . . or is it two blue with one red?'

'Perhaps you'll show us so as we can be certain?'

'Well, I . . . I suppose it's all right. I mean, me showing you when he ain't here.'

'He'd be the first to tell you to do anything that might help us find who killed his wife.'

She led the way upstairs and into a corridor which was lined with a long, built-in linen cupboard. Several of the stored blankets were straw-coloured and had two bands of red and one of blue at the top end.

'I'll take one of those,' Blundell said.

'You don't take nothing without his say-so.'

'I'll give you a receipt.'

'You'll give him the receipt, not me.'

'Very well . . . Mr Frayne doesn't have anything to worry about while you're in charge of the house!'

It was meant as a compliment, but she clearly did not receive it as such. She slid the door shut with considerably more force than was necessary.

They returned downstairs to the hall. 'Is the gardener working here now?' Blundell asked.

'Yes.'

'We'll go and have a word with him, then.'

'As you like.'

She opened the front door and stood to one side, arms crossed in front of her considerable bosom.

As they made their way round to the courtyard, Blundell said: 'I don't understand.'

'If you look at things from her point of view, she was probably right not to let us take anything away without Mr Frayne's permission . . .'

'I'm not talking about that.'

'What then?'

'That Mrs Frayne and Miss Leston maybe were . . . I mean, she was a married woman.'

'Men don't let marriage get in the way of their pleasures, so since women claim equality, I guess one shouldn't be surprised.' The detective sergeant was as square as a cube, Roach thought with amusement.

'It's been confirmed the money was all hers and now we've every reason to assume the marriage wasn't a happy one . . .' They reached the doorway through to the garden. 'I'm saying the blanket back in the house matches the one the body was wrapped up in.'

169

'Which is going to raise one very big question. How could a man who's obviously a long way from being stupid do something so completely gormless as to use one of his own blankets?'

'There's something often makes a clever man do daft things when he commits a crime – conscience, maybe. If anyone these days has one.'

Mercer was on a kneeler, hand weeding a small herbaceous border. He watched them approach.

Blundell came to a halt. 'You've met Detective Constable Roach, I think?'

There was no answer.

'We're investigating the murder of Mrs Frayne . . . A dreadful tragedy.'

'Aye.' His tone was neutral.

'This garden is looking great and it must have given Mrs Frayne great pleasure.'

'If it did, she never said as much.'

'No?'

'She'd a sight more complaints than praise.'

Blundell brought a pack of cigarettes from his pocket, offered it, struck a match. 'Not a very generous person?'

Mercer drew on the cigarette, exhaled.

'Some people are like that.'

'I said, we don't want climbers up against that.' He pointed at the brick wall which ran along the west side of the garden. "That's where I want 'em," she said, "so that's where you'll plant 'em." What happens? They gets the mould. Who did she blame? Me.'

'We've gathered she could be a bit difficult.'

'More like impossible.'

'Must have made things uncomfortable for everyone? I wouldn't mind betting her and her husband had a spat, or two?'

Mercer smoked.

'I expect you've heard 'em going on at each other?'

'If I have, I ain't talking about it.'

'Of course not. And how cheering it is in this day and age to hear someone standing up for loyalty to an employer, even when she doesn't sound like she deserved it. I've been told there were times when she went for her husband like she thought he was a nobody. That would be on account of her money, wouldn't it?'

'Would it?'

'What's he like?'

'A gentleman.'

'In the old-fashioned sense?'

'Don't know what sense. He'll talk to me like I'm the same as him, she never did.'

'Makes a big difference, doesn't it? . . . By the way, we're trying to trace a friend of Mr Frayne – unfortunately he's not here at the moment to ask – and maybe you can help us. Her name's Francesca.'

Mercer said nothing.

'She's got long red hair.'

'Never seen no redhead here.'

'I suppose you could say she's more blonde than red. Has he shown any woman around the garden recently?'

After a pause, Mercer said: 'There was the time I was mending me spade. Bought a new handle what cost a sight more'n the whole spade when it was new.'

'The price of everything rockets up. Tell me about this lady.'

'Nothing to tell. He walks her around, says in front of me I've fingers so green they'd make a desert bloom, goes back into the house.'

'I presume she was very attractive?'

'Only if you like old horses.'

'Sounds like a neigh,' Roach suggested.

'Bloody humorous!' Blundell muttered. He spoke to Mercer once more. 'D'you know what I mean by sash cord?'

171

'Yes.'

'Have you recently seen any lying about the place?'

'If something's around what shouldn't be, I pick it up. She'd only to find a small piece of paper to start bellyaching about me being blind or lazy.'

'People keep odd bits of cord and string in case they'll come in handy some day and I wondered if maybe that's what you do and perhaps you've some sash cord?'

'There's some in the hut.'

'You mean, the garden shed over there?'

'Ain't that what I've just said?'

'I'd like to have a look at the cord.'

'Why?'

'To see what it looks like.'

'Looks like sash cord. What d'you expect?'

'There are different types. So if you'd show it to us.'

Mercer led the way across to the wooden garden shed that was sited close to the eastern brick wall. He opened the door, entered. Blundell looked through the doorway to see garden machinery and equipment in apple-pie order. He watched Mercer reach up to a shelf and search its length, moving one or two things in order to do so, then bend down and look under the workbench. He straightened up. 'It ain't here,' he said, annoyed.

'Are you sure?'

He ignored a question he considered ridiculous.

'When's the last time you can be certain it was here?'

'It always is,' he answered, ignoring the fact that it wasn't.

'Was it a long length?'

'Fifteen, twenty foot. Got left over from work in the house.'

'Did it have any peculiar quality?'

'It were sash cord, that's what, and some sod's pinched it.'

Blundell and Roach returned to the courtyard to find the

Audi was now in the garage, the door of which had not been lowered.

'Looks like the lord and master is back,' Roach said.

'He may be your lord and master, but he ain't mine . . . Come on, we'll have a word. And remember, none of your stupid neighs.'

'Nay, sir, nary a one.'

'Every man a bloody comedian!'

They went on to the road and around to the front door. When Enid opened this, she said bad-temperedly, 'What now?'

'Is Mr Frayne back?'

'Yes.'

'We'd like a word with him.'

'Can't leave him alone. Don't matter to you he's just lost his wife. You've as much feeling as a dead rat.'

'As I explained earlier . . .'

She slammed the door shut.

'How to make friends without really trying,' Roach said.

Minutes later, she opened the door again. 'He says you're to come in.' Her resentment was obvious.

They entered and she directed them into the blue room. Frayne met them by the doorway. Blundell said how sorry they were to disturb him at such a sad time . . . He thanked them for their condolences, offered drinks, which were refused. 'How can I help you?' he asked, as he sat.

'Two ways, Mr Frayne,' Blundell answered. 'The first is . . . I'm very sorry I have to mention this, but your wife's body was wrapped in a blanket.'

'Well?'

'In a case like this, elimination is as important as anything . . .'

'A fact underlined by the frequency with which you, or your colleagues, mention it.'

'Quite . . . As I was saying, we need to eliminate all

173

possibilities and one of those has to be . . . If you will forgive me?'

'May I know first what it is I am asked to forgive?'

'It is fact that most murders are committed by near relatives or friends.'

Frayne was silent for a moment, then he said, his tone hardening with every word: 'Is that a roundabout way of telling me I am a suspect?'

'No, sir. To make it clear that we are as determined to prove innocence as guilt. So if you will help us do that?'

'You obviously don't take it for granted that I'll do whatever I can to assist you in identifying the murderer.'

'We do have to make certain. I mentioned the blanket earlier. One of the things we have to do in order to eliminate possibilities is make certain there are no similar blankets here, in this house.'

'To prove the negative rather than the positive is always more difficult, even if possible. But surely there's a strong possibility that the one used to . . . to wrap up my wife's body will have come from here?'

'Why do you suggest that?'

'Because they obviously needed something handy and what could have been more so?'

'There has to be that possibility,' Blundell agreed.

'So you may very well find a similar blanket; which surely will go no way to proving the negative, in other words my innocence?'

'It will show us the sequence of events.'

'A very different conclusion.'

There was a silence.

'You want to see what blankets there are in the house?'

'Yes, please, Mr Frayne.'

'Except for those in the two bedrooms, they're all in one of the cupboards.'

'If we could see them?'

They followed Frayne upstairs and for a second time

174

looked into the long cupboard in the corridor. Blundell picked out a blanket with two red stripes and one blue. 'This does look very similar, Mr Frayne.'

'Then they probably did take one from here.'

'It now certainly seems likely. May we take this back with us for comparison tests to be made at the laboratory? We will, of course, give you a receipt for it.'

'There's no reason to object.'

'Thank you, sir.' Blundell turned to Roach. 'Write out a receipt. One blanket, large size, wool, with two red stripes and one blue.'

'Do I have to apply to you for its return?' Frayne asked.

'As soon as tests are completed, we'll bring it back.'

'Will I be told the results of the tests?'

'Certainly.'

'Then if that's that, I'd rather like to be left on my own.'

'I quite understand . . . Oh, I'm afraid there is one more question. Do you know a lady by the name of Francesca?'

'Why the devil are you asking?' Frayne said angrily.

'Unfortunately, we have to find out the answers to many questions that may seem impertinent and of no relevance.'

'This has no relevance and is very impertinent.'

'Nevertheless, if you would answer?'

'I will not, since it can't possibly be of any concern to you.'

'Very well, Mr Frayne. Constable Roach has finished, so he can give you the signed receipt and we'll leave.'

As they drove away from Bell's House, Blundell said: 'That could be called one very satisfactory visit.'

'But satisfactory for whom? I still can't see him doing something as stupid as using a blanket from his own house.'

'What says he's so smart?'

'He made quick nonsense of your claim we were only trying to prove his innocence.'

'A matter of opinion,' Blundell snapped.

Twenty-One

N ewby paced between the table and the south wall of the conference room.

'Sergeant Blundell . . .' Howes began.

'Can speak for himself.'

Blundell cleared his throat. 'Roach and me went to Bell's House . . .'

'I know that. Get on with the meat, man, and stop wasting time with the gristle.'

'We spoke first to the daily, who told us Mr Frayne was not at home . . .' He nervously tried to steer a course between being too verbose in order to miss out nothing and too brief and so missing something that would evoke the detective superintendent's anger. Rank bred petty dictators.

Newby came to a halt by the window. He stared out, hands clasped behind his back. 'The blanket has gone to the lab?'

'Yes, sir,' Howes answered.

'Any marks on it?'

'One dry cleaners' tab.'

'There wasn't one on the blanket around the body?'

'That's so.'

Newby turned and spoke to Blundell. 'The sash cord that's missing from the garden shed – did you find out why it was there?'

'Mercer was keeping it in case it came in handy, sir. It was left over after work in the house at some earlier date.'

'What work?'

It was not a question Blundell had thought to put to Mercer, but it seemed there could be only one answer. 'Repairing some of the windows, sir.'

'I want a comparison section of cord taken from one of the windows that was repaired.'

'Make a note to get that done immediately,' Howes said.

'Yes, sir.' Never missed a chance to give the false impression he was sharply on the ball, Blundell thought sarcastically.

Newby crossed to the chair at the window end of the table, sat, spoke to Blundell. 'Frayne was surprised when you mentioned the name Francesca?'

'Very uptight, if you know what I mean?'

'I don't.'

'He was shocked we knew the name, sir, very annoyed that we did, and rather scared.'

'Sounds an imaginative reading of events.'

'I don't think so, sir.'

'Well, it would fit a pattern if he has a bit on the side. Where there's money, there's sex. He refused to identify who she is?'

'Yes, sir.'

'It sounds promising . . . So how do we identify her?'

'Sergeant Blundell has an idea, sir,' Howes answered quickly, determined to make certain that the result of failure would fall on the detective sergeant's shoulders, not his.

'Which is what?' Newby asked Blundell.

'The daily heard Frayne talking to someone over the phone and he called the person on the other end of the line Francesca, and it sounded like she'd a husband called Bill who was in a home because he couldn't look after himself, falling and not able to get up, and three parts gone in the head. That could all add up to Alzheimer's, even if he must be rather young to have got it. Assume Francesca lives relatively locally, then her husband will have gone into a local home.'

'Two assumptions without any viable foundations.'

'I don't know that that's right, sir.'

Newby was surprised that Blundell should have again disagreed with him, having mentally dismissed the other as an old-timer waiting for his pension and bending all his energies into keeping life peaceful. 'Why isn't it?'

'If she is Frayne's piece, he won't have had all that much free time in which to see her because of his wife, so it's likely she lives fairly close; if that's so, the home will also be close so as she can see the husband every day.'

'If Frayne's got his legs over her, she won't bother how infrequently she sees her husband.'

'My uncle had Alzheimer's and was in a home and although he never seemed to understand where he was or what he was doing, if my aunt didn't turn up each afternoon, he created trouble and that made her feel guilty.'

'Suppose you're right, then what?'

'We know the husband's name is Bill and hers is Francesca. If we make enquiries at every home within a reasonable area, we may be able to identify him, and through him, her.'

Newby stood, pushed his chair back, resumed pacing. After a while, he said, speaking as much to himself as to the other two: 'When sex and money get together, murder's always in the wings.'

'A shotgun marriage,' Howes suggested.

'This is hardly a subject for puerile humour.'

'No, sir,' Howes said, abashed.

'Question every nursing home in this division, and if that draws a blank, we'll go county-wide.'

Frayne stared with unfocused gaze at the television. Yet again, he tried to convince himself that the detectives were interested only in his innocence; yet again, he could not escape the certainty that all they had said and done pointed to their belief that he was lying and was guilty. Give a dog a bad name. They knew he'd lied to save Portia so were making the mistake of assuming once a liar, always a liar.

He stood, went through to the butler's pantry, where he poured himself the third gin and tonic of the evening. Alcohol was said to be a depressant, but without it he would be even more depressed. He returned to the blue room, changed television channels and continued not watching. They had never believed in the man in the Mickey Mouse mask or in the spray which had made him feel he was being stifled before he lost consciousness . . . He shivered. Portia had known the reality of being throttled. Panic would have exploded in her mind . . . They'd used sash cord. Mercer had told him that afternoon how the two detectives had wanted to know about the missing sash cord. They were convinced both cord and blanket had come from the house. They'd also been interested in the relationship between Portia and himself. He believed Mercer when the other claimed to have refused to discuss the matter. It was a God-awful situation, growing blacker with every minute he thought about it. The only mercy was that there was no way in which Francesca could become involved.

Timberlands was a large, graceless house built at the beginning of the twentieth century on the outskirts of Lower Brackhurst. Just inside the grandiose entrance gates was a small concrete pond with scalloped sides which had been kept empty from the day a resident had fallen into it and almost drowned in two feet of water.

Lipman rang the front door bell, marked Visitors. The door was opened by a young brunette dressed in a nurse's uniform that failed to conceal she had a shapely figure. 'Can I help you?' she asked.

She certainly could, he thought, if she was willing. 'Detective Constable Lipman, local CID—'

She interrupted him. 'Is something wrong?'

He smiled. An ex-girlfriend had told him his smile made a woman want to run her fingers through his curly hair. 'There's no call to worry, it's only a routine visit. What I'd like is a word with whoever's in charge here.'

'Mrs Hapgood's out and won't be back until the evening.'

'Then I'm sure you can tell me what I want to hear,' he said, sufficiently archly to add the intended implication.

'Depends what that is,' she answered briskly.

'I need to know if you've got a particular patient here.'

'What's the name?'

'I don't know.'

'That's a great help!'

'Suppose I come on in and explain how things are?'

When she led him through a room in which half a dozen people sat aimlessly, unconsciously conscious, he wished he had not made the suggestion. To see what the future might hold for him was to be frightened sick. They entered a small office. 'Have a chair,' she said, pointing to one at the side of the desk.

He sat. One of the women had been moving her clawed hand up and down in the air. What had she imagined she was doing? Had she any imagination left . . . ?

'Is something wrong?' she asked.

'It's just that seeing those people in there . . . Well, it makes me hope I die before I get like that.'

'Doesn't everyone?'

'Working here must depress you?'

'Occasionally. But then I remind myself I'm helping people who can't help themselves and I feel better.'

'But there must be times when you want to get away from it all and see bright lights, have fun?'

'Which I do, with my husband.'

'I was born a loser.'

'I've a job to do, so what exactly is it you want to know?'

Very bossy, he assured himself, seeking some compensation for the obvious fact she had no desire to run her fingers through his hair. 'We're trying to identify a man who's in a local nursing home. He's probably in his middle to late thirties and his Christian name is William. His wife's name is Francesca.'

She answered immediately. 'One of our patients, in his early forties, is William Price and his wife is Francesca.'

'Then it's bingo!'

'Not for either her or him.'

'Of course not,' he said contritely.

'Is that all?'

'If you'd give me her address, it will be.'

She opened the right-hand middle drawer of the desk, brought out a file and opened this. 'Thoburn Cottage, Larnhurst.'

The phone interrupted them. Lynch walked uncomfortably across to the small table on which he'd left the cordless phone; a hip was hurting and he was terrified it presaged the need for surgery. He raised the small aerial, switched on. 'Yes . . . Are you joking? . . . That's all it fetched? But I paid much more . . .' He switched off.

Ferdinand entered hurriedly. 'Is that for me, Esme, because—'

'No.'

'I'm expecting a call . . .'

'Then expect it somewhere else.'

Benson noted the look of angry resentment, touched with a vicious slyness, on Ferdinand's face as he left.

Lynch sat. 'They con you when you buy, they con you when they sell. Just bloody crooks.'

'Was this a snuff box you were selling?'

'What's it to you?'

How to make friends, Benson thought.

'So what's the set-up?'

'Like I said, the morgue's next to the coppers . . .'

'I don't pay for yesterday's news. What's the goddamn security like?'

'My contact won't talk until he sees the colour of the notes.'

'I told you, half on contract . . .'

'And I told you, it'll have to be money up front for him and the others. If you still haven't got a full wallet, you'll just have to flog some more of those things.' He looked at the nearer display cabinet.

Lynch swore.

Twenty-Two

H owes was a nervous passenger in a car and he was thankful when they turned into the drive of Thoburn Cottage; the roads would be a lot safer were the detective chief superintendent banned from driving. As the car came to a halt, he said, looking through the windscreen, 'An attractive place.'

'If you like vegetating in the countryside.' Newby opened his door and climbed out.

There were far worse ways of spending one's life than vegetating in the countryside, Howes thought. Being driven at twice the speed of safety was one of them.

Newby led the way along the brick path to the small porch, rang the bell. Francesca opened the inner door, then the outer one.

'Mrs Price?' Newby asked.

'Yes.'

'I'm Detective Chief Superintendent Newby and my companion is Detective Inspector Howes. We'd like a word with you.'

'Has there been an accident at the nursing home?'

'The one in which your husband is? As far as I know, there's been no accident there.'

'Then why are you here?'

'If we may enter, I'll explain.'

She hesitated. 'I suppose you can prove you are who you say you are?'

Newby brought out his warrant card and showed it.

'I'm sorry, but we're constantly being advised not to let anyone into the house until certain they're genuine. Please come on in.'

As they entered the sitting room, she warned them to mind their heads as they passed under the main beam. Once seated, she said: 'Perhaps now you'll explain?'

'You can't guess?' Newby said.

'Would I ask if I could?'

Good for you! Howes thought. No catwalk beauty – which in his estimation was greatly in her favour – her features suggested she would always stand up for herself.

'I understand your husband is a patient in Timberlands Nursing Home, near Lower Brackhurst?'

'Yes.'

'And he suffers from Alzheimer's?'

'What is the relevance of this?'

'Please be patient, Mrs Price. Does he often come home?'

'Never. His doctor has assured me there would be no benefit to him, probably quite the reverse, and inevitably I would find such a visit emotionally very upsetting.'

'Then you are on your own here?'

'Yes.'

'I believe you know Mr Richard Frayne?'

'Is it any of your concern whether I do or don't?'

'I think so.'

'Why?'

'Because the fact could be very pertinent.'

'I would prefer to say, impertinent.'

'Mrs Price, I assure you it will be in your interest to be helpful.'

'I will decide what is in my interest.'

'Very well. Do you know Mr Richard Frayne?'

'Yes.'

'How long have you known him?'

'Quite a while.'

'Did you first meet him before your husband became ill?'

'I can't really remember.'

'Where did you meet him?'

'At the home of mutual friends.'

'And was he with his wife?'

'Yes.'

'I'm sure you know that tragically Mrs Frayne has been murdered?'

'Of course.'

'How did you first hear that?'

'I was told by someone locally.'

'Mr Frayne?'

'No.'

'How would you have described Mrs Frayne's personality?'

'I would not try to.'

'Several people we've spoken to have said she was an emotionally cold woman.'

'Everyone has his or her own opinion.'

'But you don't have one?'

'No.'

'That's rather odd. We usually have an opinion about people we know.'

'Usually is not always.'

'Perhaps you found it more convenient not to have an opinion?'

'I don't know what you mean.'

'How would you describe the Frayne marriage?'

'It would be impertinent on my part to try to. I've no idea why you're asking these questions, but I'll be blunt, I find them insulting.'

'Why is that?'

'They suggest I pry into other people's lives.'

'Sometimes one learns about other people without deliberately prying into their lives.'

'Really?'

'Has Mr Frayne ever spoken to you about his marriage?'

'Of course not.'

'That is a subject you are both careful to avoid?'

'We observe normal social manners.'

'Does Mr Frayne often visit you here?'

'No.'

'So if someone informs us he's been here many times while your husband's been in the home, that's a lie?'

'Who has told you that?'

'I'm afraid I'm not at liberty to say. Would he come here once a week, twice a week, or more often?'

'I suppose I have been very slow. Or naive. I have always thought of the police as straightforward, honest people, but you're slyly trying to infer that Mr Frayne and I are having an affair, aren't you?'

'Are you?'

'Of course not.'

'Yet he has visited you here frequently when he's been on his own and not with his wife?'

'And you have the kind of mind that can imagine only one reason for that?'

'When an attractive woman is lonely and a man is married to someone described as an iceberg, it is very common for them to have an affair.'

'You cannot understand that someone will honour her pledge?'

'What pledge would that be?'

'The one that one makes on marriage.'

Newby smiled sarcastically. 'Words, Mrs Price, easily forgotten.'

'You don't believe there can be people who do honour them?'

'When tens of thousands of marriages end in divorce every year?'

'What is your problem? Your own marriage leads you to believe the worst?'

'You don't do yourself any good talking like that,' he said angrily.

'On the contrary, it helps to ease my resentment at your impertinence.' She stood. 'You will please leave now.'

'We will need to question you again.'

'Then perhaps you will try to show greater courtesy.' She crossed to the door and opened it.

As they drove onto the road, Newby said: 'What a bitch!'

The kind of woman, Howes thought, whom a man was lucky to know.

Frayne had told the chairman of Andrews & Sachs that he needed time off in order to come to terms with what had happened and this had immediately been granted. Now, he wondered if he'd made a mistake. With nothing definite to do, there was far too much time to think . . .

The cordless phone interrupted his bitter thoughts.

'Dick, it's Francesca.'

'I was just about to call you and suggest—'

She interrupted him. 'I've just had two visitors. Detectives.'

'What the hell did they want?'

'At first, I couldn't make that out. The older one, a detective chief superintendent, seemed to be asking questions that were irrelevant and obnoxious. Then I realized what he was getting at. He was trying to confirm you and I are having an affair.'

And he'd been fool enough to believe she could not be dragged into the case . . . 'The bastard!' he said violently.

'Twice over. He was so careless of my feelings . . . Dick, why should he make such a filthy accusation? Why did he want to know whether I thought Portia was an emotionally cold woman? What's it matter to him if your marriage was happy or unhappy?'

He picked up his glass, drank. His hand was shaking and the liquid was riffling.

'Are you still there, Dick?'

'Yes. Sorry.'

'What's happening? Why are they making such horrible suggestions?'

'Because they think I murdered Portia.'

'They what . . . Oh, my God! . . . Dick, they can't seriously think that.'

'I imagine they were never more serious.'

'But it's utterly ridiculous.'

'I know that, you know that, they don't.'

'How can they be so stupid?'

'They'd tell you they are being logical. They are justifiably convinced I lied to help Portia escape being charged with killing that woman, so they've no trouble in believing I was lying again when I told them about being woken by someone in a Mickey Mouse mask who sprayed me unconscious. What's my motive? To get her out of the way and my hands on her money. They were here yesterday when I was out and before I returned and they talked to Enid and George. How had relations been between Portia and me? Did I often bring women to the house? Had there been any sash cord lying around the place . . .'

'Why that?'

'She was throttled with sash cord.'

'Was – was there any anywhere?'

'George told them he had some in the garden shed, but when they asked him to show it to them, he couldn't find it. I returned and they demanded to look at the blankets we had and then took one away to compare it with the one in which Portia's body was wrapped up.'

'But surely they won't find anything from that?'

189

'On the contrary, I reckon it'll confirm that the one her body was in came from here.'

'Why are you so certain of that?'

'Because they've just questioned you.'

'I don't see why that follows.'

'They needed to establish and confirm a motive. And for them, the most obvious is that, as I've said, I got rid of a rich wife I didn't love in order to be with someone I did. And, God knows how, they've learned about you and have identified you as that someone.'

'It's . . . it's horrible.'

'Yes.'

'Just because we sometimes see each other, they assume we're lovers.'

'For them, it's logical in an age of wham, bam, and not even a thank you, ma'am.'

'I told the beastly superintendent I honoured my marriage vows and he had to have a nasty mind to think up such a filthy suggestion.'

'How did he react to that?'

'With scorn. Which made me feel as if he'd dragged me through slime.'

'It's he who's covered in slime.'

'What . . . what are you going to do?'

'Shelter under the umbrella of innocence.'

'When they won't begin to believe anyone? What happens if the blanket they took is exactly similar to the one Portia was wrapped up in?'

'They'll have confirmation that it came from here, which makes it much more certain that so did the sash cord. Though quite how damaging that will be, I don't know. After all, believe my story and it's very probable the men who broke in would have used whatever they found.'

'But you've told me the police don't believe anyone did break in.'

'Common sense will eventually prevail even though they are policemen.'

'How can you be facetious in the face of what's happening?'

'It helps me not get too steamed up at the thought of how much their accusations have hurt you.'

'Stop thinking of me, Dick, and worry about yourself.' She rang off without saying goodbye.

She had failed to appreciate that the true motive for his so-called facetiousness was an attempt to hide the truth from himself. He was the only suspect because the police were convinced there was no need to look for another.

Newby paced the floor of the conference room, which had become his temporary office. 'It's time to haul Frayne in for questioning.'

'He could get awkward,' Howes said.

Newby came to a stop by the table, rested his clenched fists on it, leaned forward until his arms took his weight. 'And I can get a bloody sight more awkward.'

Without even trying, Howes thought. 'What I'm getting at, sir, is that he must realize we suspect him and he may refuse to answer anything and challenge us to arrest him.'

'He'll kid himself he's too clever for us. So if we ask him here – "Just routine, Mr Frayne" – he'll cooperate right along the line, believing he's pulling the wool over our eyes . . . See it's arranged for tomorrow morning.'

'I'll speak to him myself.'

'And make certain he's on his own. There's nothing confuses things more than some grossly overpaid lawyer banging on about a witness's rights.'

Twenty-Three

They crossed the car park at the side of divisional HQ and reached the Audi. Frayne activated the remote unlocking, opened the driving door, settled behind the wheel; he inserted the key, but did not start the engine. 'There's no room for doubt.'

Clifford clipped home his seat belt. 'The detective superintendent is not what I would call a subtle man.'

'If you hadn't been there to make them think twice, they'd have arrested me and locked me up.'

'I doubt that.'

'Not when he accused me of murdering Portia?'

'He asked you if you had.'

'Where's the real difference?'

'In law, a great deal.'

'Can't they understand that whatever our relationship was, I couldn't have so much as hit her, let alone murdered her?'

'One has to remember that inevitably when there's a crime, they suffer the need to identify a criminal as soon as possible.'

'I did not kill Portia. How in the hell am I going to make them believe that?'

'It's going to be more a question of disproving their assertions. Broadly speaking, all the evidence against you they've quoted is circumstantial. There's the hackneyed saying that witnesses can lie, circumstances cannot, but that's true only in so far as it goes. Conclusions need to be drawn from circumstances and they can be very wrong.'

Frayne started the engine. As he backed the car, Clifford coughed, a frequent mannerism when he feared that what he was about to say might distress his client. 'There are some facts the police haven't yet introduced and need to be examined before they do.'

'Such as?'

'Were you aware that Mrs Frayne frequently changed her will?'

'Not specifically.' Frayne drove out on to the road. 'But if I'd annoyed her, usually by not doing what she wanted, she'd threaten to leave everything to a dog's home. A cat's home would have been more in character.'

'Hardly a wise remark. You would be advised to remember that "Veritas odium parit".'

'I might, if I knew what it meant.'

'Truth breeds hatred. Or to put it more freely, there are times when it's wise not to be frank to one's friends, let alone one's enemies.'

'Point taken.'

'We have to accept that the prosecution would make considerable play of the fact that at the time of Mrs Frayne's death you were the main beneficiary under her will, but that she was contemplating changing that.'

'My God! Something I knew nothing about, but which can place a noose around my neck.'

'If hanging had not been abolished,' Clifford said pedantically. 'You are – or to be more accurate, would be – a wealthy man provided . . . You wish me to be frank?'

'From the way you ask, probably not. But I guess you'd better be.'

'Under the law, a convicted criminal may not benefit from his crime.'

'You're presuming I'm to be arrested, charged, and convicted. That really boosts my morale!'

'I'm presuming nothing. I am trying to make certain you appreciate the true picture.'

'Is there such a thing as truth?'

'It is whatever the jury believes . . . Do you know the extent of Portia's estate?'

'It was always kept a dark secret.'

'Excluding the house and contents, her total investments amount roughly to two and a half million pounds. Do you have much capital of your own?'

'None at all.'

'Then unfortunately, the possible motive of greed is strong. Added to which, you are friendly with Mrs Price and—'

'And that does not, repeat not, mean I'm jumping into her bed. To be frank, I'd like to, but she will never betray her marriage even though her husband wouldn't know if she was bedding half the countryside.'

'You have frequently visited her at her home?'

'It depends what you mean by "frequently"?'

'The prosecution would claim that however often, it was frequently . . . Have you always been on your own when you've visited her house?'

'Portia hasn't usually been with me.'

'Usually or never?'

'The first time we went to Thoburn Cottage we went together.'

'After that, you were careful she was not with you?'

'Portia wouldn't go since they didn't like each other.'

'A relationship best left unstated since dislike between ladies frequently stems from jealousy.'

They stopped for lights.

'You do realize, Dick, what the average person thinks when he's told that a man married to a woman for whom he no longer has an affection . . .'

'Who's going to confirm that?'

'From the questions you were being asked back at the

station, it's clear the police have evidence that at the very least relations between you and Portia were not of the happiest.'

'Enid's probably heard Portia going at me.' The lights changed and he drove forward.

'And your replying in kind?'

'Whatever I've said, I've never threatened her.'

'Would you accept that occasionally you probably spoke very heatedly?'

'No.'

'Would a listening daily perhaps be less certain?'

'God knows what Enid has said or will say. If she describes a christening you could think she's talking about a wake.'

'If evidence is presented in court that your marriage was not of a warm, loving nature – the fact that you are relatively young yet slept in separate bedrooms could be made to seem pertinent – and that when on your own you visited a lady whose husband is in a nursing home, the jury almost inevitably are going to be ready to assume you were having an affair.'

'They maybe won't believe me when I deny that, but they'll believe Francesca.'

'When a person is clearly shown to have a reason for lying, it becomes much more difficult to believe in the veracity of that person.'

'What's that add up to in plain language?'

'Sooner or later, regrettably, Mrs Price's husband will die and clearly she will be left in very reduced circumstances. If you are not charged with murder, or are charged and found not guilty, you will inherit a very large sum of money.'

'You'd make Christ seem a liar.'

'I am a lawyer,' he replied.

Francesca opened the outside door and, her deep blue eyes expressing concern, said: 'Is this sensible?'

'Probably not,' Frayne replied.

She moved aside to let him pass through to the triangular hall. She closed the door. 'Then why come here?'

'Like a little boy who's lost his way, I want sympathy and a large gin.'

'You must have had an unusual boyhood . . . Go on in and pour two gins.'

In the sitting room, he crossed to the cocktail cabinet, poured out two drinks, slumped down in a chair, stared at the inglenook fireplace and wondered if in the past there had been someone who sat in it, warming himself and his ale, frightened because he could see catastrophe ahead yet could find no way of escaping it.

She entered, settled on the settee with her legs tucked under her as she so often did. 'Has something more happened?'

'I had to go to the police station this morning to be questioned by the detective in charge.'

'That horrible superintendent?'

'I can think of a far stronger description. He asked me to help him in his enquiries and then before I had time to answer, informed me that not to do so would arouse suspicion.' He drank. 'How can one arouse suspicion when it is already up and shouting?'

'Dick, you're not making much sense.'

'Then I'm adapting to circumstances . . . I did not murder Portia, but from the way the police are behaving, it's quite clear that they aren't looking anywhere else.'

'Why are they so certain you're guilty?'

He explained.

'Surely your solicitor could have done a hell of a lot more to make them understand how wrong they are?'

'Clifford worked hard, but if he spoke the truth – which he'd never do for fear of being sent to Coventry by his fellow practitioners—'

'Why can't you ever stop being facetious?'

'Because it's my way of hiding the fact that I'm in a blue funk. All the evidence is circumstantial, but it seems to point only at me. Portia was wealthy and was about to remove me from her will, I've often visited you on my own, so in a page-three world, it's too obvious for words – we're rumpling the bedclothes . . . Why can't they understand a man and woman can be friends and nothing more?'

She lowered her glass. 'Dick . . . The other day when I was feeling very low and you were here, I suggested you didn't have to leave, but stayed longer. Did you wonder if I was really suggesting you stayed the night?'

'I respect you too much to think that . . .' He paused. 'I'm a bloody liar! Of course I wondered. And regretfully came to the immediate conclusion you weren't.'

'You would have liked to stay?'

'I'd have offered my soul to the devil for the chance.'

'Then the police's presumption that we're having an affair isn't so absurd, is it?'

'Yes it is, because they are seeing everything through blinded eyes. Nothing will persuade them we haven't been having a very torrid affair because they cannot conceive how much you treasure loyalty. To them, that sort of loyalty has become a joke.'

'Is it this which makes them so certain you killed Portia?'

'In part. Her wealth is the other part.'

'If it were just her wealth, they wouldn't be so certain?'

'Perhaps not. But I have to face what is, not what might be.'

'You think there really may be a trial?'

'Clifford wouldn't admit it, but he reckons that's almost certain.'

'If the worst comes to the worst and you are tried, it won't matter what the police believe, will it? It's what the jury will believe? And they're just ordinary people, not conditioned to think the worst of others, not presuming circumstances always arrow the right direction, but who are ready to allow that emotion can be genuine.'

'Where's this leading to?'

She stood. 'Have you eaten?'

He looked up at her. 'Why do I get the impression you're thinking of doing something I'd veto?'

'I've no idea why you imagine you can veto any decision of mine.' She walked past him and went out into the hall, then turned and spoke through the doorway. 'You didn't say whether you've eaten?'

He shook his head. 'I dropped Clifford at his office and drove straight here.'

'Do you like Spanish omelette?'

'Very much.'

She turned back and walked off, passing out of sight.

He wished he could log into the thoughts that were obviously swirling around in her mind.

Dennis the Menace earned his ridiculous nickname not for appearance or manner, but for his ability to neutralize the most advanced of alarm systems. The other three, hiding as best they could in the shadows, very conscious of the close proximity of the police station, planned their independent escape routes should Dennis for once make a mistake and the alarms sound. All four considered their task absurd, but five thousand pounds each for a job that, apart from the alarms and the proximity of the police station, was a doddle, made absurdity attractive.

There was a low whistle. The alarm system was now inoperative.

There were no windows – the public had to be spared the possibility of stomach-churning sights – and they could use torches without the fear of revealing their presence. They passed through the PM room, in the

centre of which were two stainless-steel operating tables
under light pods, and entered the storage space – a room,
one wall of which consisted of large cabinets so that it
looked like an overgrown unit for left luggage.

Palmer read the card which was slotted into the holder
on the front of each locker and when he reached the last
one on the bottom row, straightened up.

'Which is it?' Torrents asked.

'It ain't any.'

'There's got to be. Check again.'

Palmer swore, read the cards a second time. 'Like I
bleeding well said, she ain't here.'

'Some lazy bastard hasn't written her name. Get the
stiffs out to make certain.'

'You know what she looks like?'

'Yeah.'

It took time to open each locker, slide out the inner
tray, fold back the white sheet, check which contained a
woman, and then study her face. Life had anaesthetized
all of the intruders, yet the chill from the lockers, the
frozen faces with their grimaces of death, had each one
wishing himself elsewhere.

'He's out of luck,' one of them said.

'And so will we bloody well be if we don't find the
bitch. There must a record of deliveries. Find it.'

In a built-in cupboard in the wall opposite the cabinets
there were various files and papers, amongst which was
a ledger that recorded arrivals and departures. Carol
Fowler had been there, but had been removed very
recently.

Torrents threw the book onto the floor in a gesture of
impotent rage.

They left.

Twenty-Four

N ewby was talking over the phone when Howes entered
the conference room. Where another man would have
gestured with his hand to tell the DI to sit, he did not. A
couple of minutes later, he slammed down the receiver.
'Not an ounce of initiative amongst the lot of 'em.' He
looked up. 'Well?'

'Mrs Price is down in the front room and asking to speak
to you.'

'I'll be damned! Like a bet on what's brought her
here?'

'I'm not really a betting man.'

'Can't say you look like one,' Newby said sarcastically.
'She's here because she's scared that if she goes on lying,
she'll be in big trouble. I've always said, nothing is better
at making a witness speak the truth than sweating time.
If I don't have the evidence to bring a case inside the
next half-hour, I'll donate my pension to out-of-work
layabouts . . . Go down, take her into one of the interview
rooms, and say she'll have to wait until I'm free. If she
wants to talk, discourage her. There's nothing like more
silence to jangle the nerves.'

Howes left and went down to the front room. Francesca
was sitting at a small table on which were out-of-date
magazines.

'Good morning, Mrs Price. I don't know if you remember me—'

'Of course I do,' she interrupted. 'Inspector Howes.'

'Would you like to come along to the interview room?'

He led the way across the front room, along a passage, and into the first of the interview rooms. 'I'm afraid the chairs aren't very comfortable, Mrs Price.'

'I'm well padded,' she said with a quick smile.

She was an attractive woman, he confirmed to himself as he sat opposite her at the oblong table on the wall side of which was a tape recorder. Not beautiful, but attractive, with considerable character imprinted in her face. The last time she'd faced Newby, she'd held her own – he hoped she'd do so again. She possessed a quality, difficult to determine, which aroused sympathy. 'The superintendent will be down just as soon as he's free.' Newby had told him to discourage talk, but he was damned if he was going to let her sit there in silence in what half resembled a cell – walls painted in institutional brown and bare except for a framed list of witnesses' rights, barred window high up, the only furniture the table and four chairs. 'Would you like some coffee?'

'I don't think so, thanks.'

He said the weather had been nice, hadn't it? Did she often drive down to the coast? When it was fine, he often went down with the family, but the sea was really too cold for pleasurable swimming. She asked him about his family. He proudly told her how his younger son was doing so well at university that everyone was hoping he'd get a two one, or maybe even a first.

Newby came in and briefly his expression showed his annoyance at finding a pleasant conversation in progress. He said a curt good morning, turned to Howes. 'We'll start.'

Howes switched on the tape recorder. 'Thursday, the twenty-first of September. The time is eleven sixteen in the morning. Present is Mrs Price, who lives at Thoburn Cottage, Larnhurst, and she is here at her own request. Also present are Superintendent Newby and Inspector Howes.'

Newby said: 'Mrs Price, would you now say what it is
you wish to tell us?' He carefully spoke in neutral tones.
It was not impossible, just difficult, to judge from a tape
recording when the interrogating officer had shown an
overbearing, bullying manner.

'When you were at my house the other day and asked
me questions, I did not . . .'

'Yes, Mrs Price?'

'I kind of lied.'

'In respect of what?'

'I told you I had never . . . never been very friendly
with Dick.'

'Is "Dick" Mr Richard Frayne?'

'Yes.'

'By "very friendly", do you mean sexual intercourse?'
There was a long pause. 'Yes,' she murmured.

'Please speaker louder.'

'Yes.'

'Are you now admitting that you have had sexual intercourse with Mr Frayne?'

'Must you put it so crudely?'

'Mrs Price, it will be much better if we speak in direct
terms. Sexual intercourse is a term which can be, and is,
clearly defined. I will ask you again. Are you now admitting
that you have had sexual intercourse with Mr Frayne?'

'Yes.'

'When did sexual intercourse with him first take place?'

'Two nights ago.'

'What?' Newby said, his voice high.

'Tuesday night.'

'Are you now saying you did not have sexual intercourse
with Mr Frayne previous to this Tuesday?'

'Yes.'

'You have been friendly with him for a long time and
he has visited your house when you have been on your
own . . .'

'If you're trying to suggest we made love prior to two nights ago, you don't understand.'

'Did Mrs Frayne ever accompany Mr Frayne when he visited you?'

'Only once that I can remember.'

'And you saw no reason for Mr Frayne's not visiting you in circumstances which might be thought damaging to your reputation?'

'No.'

'Many people would.'

'Only if they're incapable of envisaging a relationship of which the basis is ordinary friendship.'

'Experience suggests that such a friendship as yours soon becomes sexual in nature.'

'That must depend on the type of experience one has had.'

'Mrs Price, do you wish to maintain that you and Mr Frayne did not have sexual intercourse before this Tuesday evening?'

'Isn't that what I keep saying?'

'It is hard to believe.'

'The truth often can be.'

'There are lies which are even harder to believe.'

'If I explain, you may be able to understand I am not lying.'

'Then perhaps you'll try to explain.'

'Before Bill went into a home, we met Dick and Portia. We both instinctively liked him, but were not so sure about her. And when she came to Thoburn Cottage for cocktails, it became very clear that she decided we were not worth bothering with – we lived in a small house and obviously weren't well off since Bill had had to stop working. We weren't asked again to Bell's House, which certainly didn't worry us, but Dick used to drop in from time to time and we both liked to see him. Then Bill's illness became rapidly worse and I just couldn't cope with his being at home any longer and he had to go into a nursing home. Dick asked if he could continue to call and I said yes because seeing him was good for my morale—'

Newby interrupted her. 'Did your husband know that Mr Frayne was continuing to visit you at your home?'

'Naturally I told him, but whether or not he understood, I can't be certain. It's very difficult, often impossible, to judge how much he appreciates.'

'You saw no reason for Mr Frayne not visiting you when you were on your own?'

'Because I honoured the vow I took at my marriage – as I have said to you before.'

'Did he ever make an advance?'

'Did he try to make love to me? No. Did he want to? Yes.'

'How could you know that if he did not attempt to do so?'

'With all your undoubted experience, you must real-ize that a woman almost always knows when a man desires her.'

'Knowing he desired you, you still allowed him to visit you at your house when you were on your own?'

'Yes.'

'Did you not think that, the circumstances being what they were, your action might cause people to believe you were having an affair with him?'

'I never concern myself with what nasty-minded people do or don't think. I knew I was not betraying my marriage, however much I was tempted.'

'You admit you were tempted?'

'To be desired is almost as strong an aphrodisiac as to desire.'

'But you were able to resist the temptation until two nights ago. I find that difficult to believe.'

'Perhaps you do not hold to the same standards as I do.'

'Or perhaps I have more intelligence than you wish to credit me with,' he snapped, immediately regretting this brief verbal display of anger.

'Shall I continue?' she asked.

'I thought you'd concluded.'

'Then you understand even less about human nature than I thought. I was at home, making some woollen toys for sale at the village fête at the end of the month, when Dick arrived and was in such an emotionally confused state that it was some time before I could get him to explain what had happened. He told me how a man dressed in a mask had broken into the house and rendered him unconscious with a spray; that when he'd come to, he'd found Portia was missing . . .'

'He arrived at your house and told you all this had happened the previous night?'

'Yes.'

'And you have described him as being in an emotionally disturbed state?'

'I said "confused", but disturbed will probably do.'

'Had he driven to your house?'

'Of course.'

'A person in a state of shocked emotions is normally incapable of driving anywhere.'

'If you're right, Dick obviously proved himself the exception.'

'What did you do when he arrived at your house?'

'What anyone would do in such circumstances, my best to help him. Which was almost nothing because he couldn't stop worrying about what awful things might have happened to Portia.'

'What did he fear?'

'How am I supposed to know exactly what went on in his mind? Judging by his distress, he was imagining she was suffering every ghastly thing he'd ever heard or read about.'

'Would you describe him as overcome by fear?'

'That would not be an exaggeration.'

'Yet he drove from his home to yours?'

'You keep querying that.'

'Because I find it very difficult to believe that a man in the mental state you describe would be able to drive anywhere.'

'I can only tell you what happened.'

'But is it the truth?'

'Yes.'

'What did he do after you'd helped him as much as you could?'

'Said he must return to his place to know if Portia had been found and left. I phoned him later and he seemed more composed, but on Sunday he told me Portia's body had been found in Steelwater Lake and he was in an even worse state.'

'Where was he when he told you that?'

'In his home. He phoned to tell me.'

'You would claim to be able to judge his emotional state over the phone?'

'When a man has difficulty in speaking coherently, you don't imagine he's perfectly calm.'

'It's easier to fake an emotion over the phone than face to face.'

'You believe a man has to fake his grief when his wife has been found murdered?'

'Did he visit you that day?'

'No.'

'One would have expected him to since you claim to have previously been able to help him overcome his emotions. When did he next visit you?'

'On Tuesday evening. He was hardly in control of himself.'

'Yet he managed to drive from his place to yours.'

'Have you been lucky enough never to have had to

drive when your mind has been in a maelstrom? . . . He was probably a danger to everyone else on the road, but he got to my place. Do you know why he was in so terrible an emotional state?'

'Tell me.'

'Because you so obviously believed he had murdered Portia. Time and again, he asked me how anyone could be so cruelly wrong. It wasn't the happiest of marriages, but he'd never lifted a finger to her. The pain of your unjust, ridiculous accusation on top of Portia's murder and the frightening experience he'd suffered in Bell's House had all but flipped his reason. At one point he was virtually hysterical, threatening to commit suicide because he couldn't face things any longer.'

'Did you call for medical help?'

'I decided there was only one way in which he could be helped. I took him to my bed.'

'Even though you put so much store in honouring your marriage vows?'

'You find it easy to sneer. I hope you never have the misfortune to be faced with the situation I was. I liked Dick very much; since I'm telling the truth, I'll admit I could easily let myself love him. And there he was, in such a state of mental confusion and pain that he was talking about suicide. Yet I knew I could bring him a measure of calm if I broke my vows and let him make love to me.'

'How could you know that?'

'Does something have to be in capital letters before you can read it? I knew! So I told myself that Bill would understand that I would be helping someone out of a mental hell and not succumbing to my own desires and I took him to bed. And I thank God that I was able to give him calm.'

'Suppose I tell you I do not believe a word of what you're telling me?'

'I cannot control your belief or disbelief, I can only tell you what actually happened and, for my own sake, try to explain why it did.'

'Have you anything more you wish to tell us?'

'No.'

'Then the interview is over.'

Howes switched off the recorder. Francesca stood, Howes did the same, Newby remained seated. Howes accompanied her to the outer door. She looked as if she were gathering up her thoughts to speak to him at some length, then restricted herself to a brisk goodbye. She walked away.

He returned to the interview room where Newby was still seated. 'Shall I rewind the tape and log it, sir?'

'Throw it into the bloody dustbin . . . She must have graduated with honours from RADA. Shall I tell you something – she even had me ready to believe her.'

'I must say I thought . . .'

'I don't give a toss what you thought.' Newby finally came to his feet. He began to pace the floor, having continually to turn because the room was small. 'When she kept claiming she'd honoured her marriage until she sacrificed her virtue not for her own pleasure, but to help someone else, I could almost see a halo gathering around her head . . . Can you imagine how a jury would respond to her?'

'It's difficult to judge . . .'

'Nothing is bloody easier. Defence makes certain there are more women than men on the jury because women revere sacrifices, most especially when it's one of them sacrificing herself for the man she loves. The women will refuse to believe she and Frayne have been screwing almost from the day they met; they'll accept he didn't stone her cherry until he turned up so distraught she had to crown him with beaver or he'd commit suicide; they'll listen aghast as she cons them into believing he was so

208

distraught because we were cruelly stupid and believed he'd murdered his wife.'

'Then where do we go from here?'

'We send the papers to the CPS and to cover ourselves give it as our opinion that in view of that bitch's evidence there is so little chance of proving the truth and gaining a conviction that it cannot be in the public's interest to bring the case.'

Twenty-Five

'They say what?' Lynch demanded furiously.

'The body wasn't there,' Benson replied nervously.

'When I pay heavy for information that turns out to be shit . . .'

'Esme, it was in that mortuary, like I told you. Only with Mrs Frayne dead – which you wanted – things changed and someone gave some money anonymously so as Carol's daughter could see her mother given a proper funeral and that's what's happened.'

'So they planted her out. Find out which cemetery.'

'I've tried.'

'Then try again and this time you'd better succeed.'

'But I know where she is.'

'Then why can't you sodding well say so? Get a team to dig her up before she's had time to ripen.'

'She's not in a grave.'

'You're annoying me!' Lynch shouted.

'It's like this. Someone spoke to the friend who was looking after Carol's kid and she said Carol had often told her how she didn't want to be buried when she died.'

'So?'

'She was cremated.'

'Then find who's got the ashes . . .'

'It's no good, Esme. They say that because diamonds are pure carbon they'll have burned up in the cremation.' Benson stood. 'Sorry things have worked out like this, but there's nothing anyone can do now. I've got to move.' He hurried out of the house. He did not want to be around when Lynch's backers discovered they were not going to be paid the capital and interest owed.

Newby, who was standing by the table in the conference room, said: 'Yes?'

Roach stepped further into the room. 'Inspector Howes said to give you a report that's just in, sir.'

'What is it?'

'They think there might have been a break-in at the mortuary last night.'

Newby straightened up, a single sheet of paper in his right hand. 'What the hell's "might have been" supposed to mean?'

'It seems that in the morning the log listing dates of body arrivals and departures was on the floor, but the mortuary assistant is quite certain he put it in the cupboard the previous night. And the log was a long way from where it could have fallen from a working surface, it was face downwards and open, and the state of the pages suggests it landed with far more force than if it had just fallen. They reckon it could have been thrown down by whoever broke in.'

'Is there an alarm system?'

'A good one. But after finding the log, they checked and there was some indication that it might have been bypassed.'

'How many more goddamn "might have beens" are they going to serve up? Maybe they'd like to explain why a mob sufficiently experienced to queer the alarms would break into a morgue.'

'They don't try to give an opinion as to that.'

'Of course they don't.'

'But I think I can suggest why, sir.'

'You do, do you? Then make it quick because I'm in a hurry.'

'I asked for a check to be made on what bodies had recently been in store. One was Carol Fowler's. Whoever broke in could have been looking for her.'

'Why?'

'I remember something in the report on her daughter. She was questioned to see if she knew anything that might help explain her mother's recent movements and identify the man in the car. She said her mother had been in Africa; when asked where, she named somewhere called Town.'

'Very helpful!'

'But suppose she meant Freetown? Suppose Carol was being used as a mule to bring in illegally mined diamonds. At the airport, her minder picked up a car to drive her to wherever she was to stay until the diamonds appeared. Along the way, the car suffered a puncture; she got out and was on the road when a Mercedes driven by a drunken Mrs Frayne ran her down and killed her. She ended up in the mortuary and obviously was going to stay there until a case was brought against the driver of the car. We identified Mrs Frayne, but couldn't collect enough evidence to charge her. The big man somehow learned her identity and, realizing he had to move things on before he could recover the diamonds, organized the raid on Bell's House during which Mrs Frayne was snatched and later murdered, amidst a raft of clues that would make us believe her husband was the murderer – necessary, or we might start wondering about motive. Mrs Frayne's death brought to an end the need to keep Carol's body on ice and everything should have moved forward smoothly for the big man. But what he had not allowed for was that events would move so swiftly that when the mortuary was broken into, Carol's body was already away. And she had not been buried, but cremated.'

Newby shut his case. 'With an imagination so out of control, you ought to be in the bloody government.'

* * *

Frayne, waiting in Thoburn Cottage, heard Francesca drive into the yard and rushed out of the house. She had garaged the car and opened the driving door by the time he reached her. 'Well?' he said breathlessly.

She stepped out of the car, shut the door. 'He was certain I was lying, but although he tried to hide the fact, was obviously so angry that I think I may just have managed it.'

They walked down to the gate, along the brick path to the small porch, and into the house 'There's a bottle of Veuve Clicquot waiting in the refrigerator,' he said.

'If only we could be certain we would be drinking to success.'

She went into the sitting room and he collected the bottle and two glasses, joined her. He filled the glasses, handed her one. 'I want to thank you as I've never thanked anyone before, only I just can't find the words.'

'You don't have to speak for me to hear.'

'You betrayed yourself for my sake.'

'Only in words.'

'Don't try to make out it didn't hurt like hell – knowing you were confirming the lie they believed.'

'Of course it hurt. But if it's saved you, it will have been worth every slice of pain.'

He raised his glass. 'To you.'

'But I can't drink a toast to myself.'

He drank. 'Now you won't be.'

'Dick—' She abruptly stopped.

'Is something up?'

'There's something I want to say . . .'

He waited.

'I think I've crossed a kind of bridge.' She played with the stem of the glass, twisting it between finger and thumb as she stared down at it. 'When I saw Bill yesterday, he didn't begin to recognize me. It's the first time things have been that bad and it shocked me. The matron saw how upset I was and said, "He's not the man you married, Mrs Frayne; that man left the body some time ago." She was trying to help me come to terms with the situation, but at the time I was just furiously dismayed by what I saw as complete crassness. But returning from seeing the detectives just now, I began to see that she was right. Bill isn't the man I married; he has gone away and can never return. So I . . .' She drank. When she next spoke, she did so hurriedly. 'I'm trying to say that if you want to, stay the night here.'

'There's nothing I want more.' He paused. 'But have you really crossed that bridge? Can you cross it whilst Bill is still alive, whether he knows you, or doesn't? If we made love it would be wonderful, but when you next visited Bill, maybe you'd feel guilty. You value loyalty so highly that perhaps you never could in your heart see a relationship between us as anything but disloyalty.'

She drained her glass. 'You're the first man I've propositioned. And what happens?'

After a long while, he said: 'I don't know.'

'And goddamnit, nor do I!'